MEN & WOMEN

Edited by Paul Burston

GLASSHOUSE BOOKS

CONTENTS

LUCKY PATRICIA

LUCKY PATRICIA

VG LEE

I'd agreed to meet Jan for lunch at the Dragon Bar in the old town. We'd be joined by our mutual American friend Patricia and her new girlfriend Dawn, also American. Patricia is the kind of woman who makes flying visits. Suddenly she's in the country and if I'm not quick about it, she's flown off somewhere else and I've missed her for another two years.

She keeps in touch by round-robin emails, but not tedious ones. No, *Monica's kittens are unbelievably cute or Guess what? We've succumbed to a gas barbecue!* Patricia's round-robins are full of sex and suicide. Nobody she knows ever just breaks up with their partner and walks off into the sunset; wrists are slashed, cars are trashed, vendettas form, litigation lasts, which brings excitement-at-a-safe-distance into my quiet life as a small scale market gardener.

Dawn, the new girlfriend, first surfaced about eight months ago; a brief mention when she joined Patricia's book group. A fortnight later and she'd arrived at Patricia's flat in tears – at two am and with several large, expensive suitcases. Jefferson, (Dawn's husband) had 'sworn on his mother's life to behead Dawn with the axe he kept for chopping firewood.'

'This guy is the Director of a Multi-National,' Patricia wrote, 'He's willing to jeopardise his whole career to wipe poor Dawn off the face of the earth. Can you believe it?'

Well no, I hadn't quite believed it. My own thoughts were that he was probably just very annoyed with Dawn, perhaps because she'd joined a lesbian book group, but once he calmed down they would work things out over a nice meal and a bottle of good wine which as a Director of a Multi-National he could well afford. Or they might just divorce and live happily ever after. I set aside the question of just what was the Director of a Multi-National doing chopping his own firewood in the first place?

By Easter, Jefferson had disappeared from Patricia's emails but Dawn was mentioned frequently. Dawn smelt 'like a bowl of expensive, ripe peaches'. I liked the words bowl, expensive and peaches but was uncertain about 'ripe' but that could have been due to my horticultural background. 'Ripe' meant 'action stations' because quite quickly after ripe comes 'over-ripe'. Before I could dwell too much on this another email arrived telling me (and all the rest of Patricia's friends world-wide) that Dawn's underwear was 'to die for'.

'My personal favourites are her silk French knickers and camisole top ensemble in eau de nil,' Patricia informed us, 'Never in my life have I met a woman wearing eau de nil underwear. Eat your hearts out, guys.'

At that point Jan and I met up to compare reactions.

I said, 'It would take far more than Dawn's underwear ensemble to make me willing to kill myself on its behalf Jan, although I must admit I have re-assessed my own underwear drawer and found it wanting.'

Jan frowned. 'Lucy, I think you've missed the point here – what Patricia is actually telling us, is that she and Dawn are now lovers.'

'Are they?'

'Well how else would she know about Dawn's underwear?'

'Perhaps she saw them drying over Dawn's towel rail.'

'Do rich people dry their underwear over towel rails?' Jan asked as if she really wanted to know.

Of course she was right about them being lovers. By Christmas we had personal facts about Dawn at our fingertips we didn't know about each other and Jan and I had been friends for nearly fifteen years. Quite apart from Dawn's recent tattoo of the Tree of Life, its roots curling down between the 'firm globes of Dawn's buttocks', Dawn also owned a Lichtenstein and several Pollocks, a weekend house in Key West and took her long holidays in Bermuda, Dawn was apartment hunting but she'd not found anything with enough space to do her art collection justice.

I had a bad feeling about Dawn that I didn't share with Jan who tries very hard to be a glass-half-full woman, notwithstanding her rocky long term relationship with Eileen a local dog breeder. I think it was Dawn's money that gave me the bad feeling. Well yes, it was definitely her money.

I'm not poor. Nor am I rich. I never will be. Not that kind of rich that owns chunks of New York and works of art. I hoped my bad feeling wasn't about envy but more anxiety for Patricia's welfare. It seemed as if she'd attached herself to a jet plane, (Dawn). I visualised Patricia in a leather flying helmet and goggles hanging on to one of Dawn's sleek, gleaming wings, exhilarated, intoxicated, not realising the danger she might be in.

I found Jan already sitting in the Dragon Bar with a glass of wine. She'd pulled up four chairs around an oval table near the door. Patricia and Dawn were coming down from London by train and weren't sure of their exact time of arrival so Jan had brought along two fleece jackets to put over the backs of the vacant chairs.

'It gets so crowded at lunchtime – I'd hate Patricia and Dawn not to have seats.'

'We could all stand at the bar.'

'I can't imagine Dawn would enjoy standing at the bar. She is a multi-millionairess.'

'Is she?'

'If she owns real estate …'

Sometimes Jan's thoughtfulness amazes me. It goes well beyond and above normal thoughtfulness. It's as if most of her day is spent devising little extra kindnesses for everyone that often go unnoticed or unappreciated. Jan has a nice face. Her eyes are her best feature. They are brown and warm and objectively would look perfectly at home in a Labrador's head which is possibly why Eileen the dog breeder took up with Jan in the first place.

Outside it was a beautiful sunny April day which made the interior of the bar seem particularly dark. We lit four tee lights.

'Welcoming,' Jan said.

I was in good spirits and although Jan seemed a little down, we both agreed we were curious about Dawn and it would be great to see Patricia again. I kept our conversation off the loathsome Eileen who was having an affair with a woman called Joyce who bred Bedlington Terriers.

'I have to admit that they are lovely little dogs,' Jan had told me earlier in the week, as if that were sufficient reason for Eileen to prefer Joyce, 'like lambs.'

'They're perfectly horrible little dogs – they're like lambs that have walked into a wall.'

'Which makes them rather endearing, don't you think? Vulnerable.'

There are moments when Jan is so sweet natured I almost find myself applauding Eileen's bad behaviour.

I ordered a glass of white wine for myself and regaled Jan with tales of my new asparagus bed, my setback with Chinese Artichokes counter-balanced by my outstanding success with Dwarf Cannellino Beans.

'I've never heard of Cannellino Beans,' she said admiringly.

'I'll let you have some of my seedlings.'

'Perhaps we could swap – my courgette seedlings for your beans?'

I didn't really need Jan's courgette seedlings but we agreed on a seedling exchange at the weekend over a glass of wine on my patio weather permitting, which sounded quite fun. Days spent working with the soil are often rewarding but can get lonely.

Jan touched my arm. 'They're here.'

Patricia and Dawn stood in the doorway as if reluctant to step out of the sunlight. The two of them formed an attractive tableau against the backdrop of old town Elizabethan shop fronts. They were exactly the same height, about five foot three and they faced each other. Patricia was smiling at Dawn and Dawn was staring directly into Patricia's eyes in an adult kind of way.

Jan jumped to her feet and called out, 'Hey, you two. Hurry up, we're starving.' I stood up as well and shouted, 'Ditto.'

They started laughing at something each saw in the other's eyes, then Patricia took Dawn's hand and led her in.

Dawn was very slender, very straight backed. She was probably nearing fifty but with not an ounce of extra flesh. I envied her, her jaw line. I wondered if she'd had surgery but decided not. We lesbians don't often do surgery. Not that Dawn looked like any lesbian I'd ever met. She made me think of a predatory bird or a very thin, sleek wolf. She wore jeans, leather, Cuban heeled boots, an expensive looking puffa jacket with a drawstring waist which as a rule flatters no one but on Dawn it actually looked good.

Patricia helped her slip out of the jacket draping it over Jan's fleece on the back of the chair. For all Dawn's leanness her figure was womanly, high full breasts emphasised by the snug fit of her scarlet polo-neck.

'Thank you for that darling,' Dawn said to Patricia as if hanging up her jacket had been at least as arduous as say, bringing life-saving water from a distant oasis. She sat down. We didn't sit. Patricia introduced us. It felt like being presented to royalty. I hopped nervously from one foot to another not knowing whether to plant a kiss either on Dawn's face or in the air around her face or just drop a low curtsey. Finally I settled on sticking my hands in the pockets of my trousers, smiling as widely as my lips would allow and nodding my head.

'Hey.' Patricia punched me gently in the ribs.

'Hey.' I hugged her.

'I've told Dawn so much about you guys.'

Jan and I beamed at Dawn. I didn't respond with, 'And Patricia's told us so much about you Dawn,' in case Dawn leant interestedly forward and asked, 'Yeah? What'd she tell you?'

'Oh just about your Tree of Life tattoo, your buttocks, your underwear and your husband wanting to behead you. The usual.'

Jan went to the bar and came back with a bottle of Dry House White and four glasses, then went back for Still Bottled Water and two water glasses because Patricia and Dawn were still feeling a 'little nauseous' from the repetitive movement of the train. While Jan poured wine and water and had to be restrained from going in search of ice cubes I studied Dawn.

Her hair was black relieved by fine threads of grey. A perfect cut, a naturally wavy Greek-boy statue style. A garland of laurel would have been appropriate or any garland. I found myself tracing the outline of Dawn's top lip on the thigh of my trousers. Her lip was thin but again perfect, two peaks with a dip carved between. Sharp cheekbones, a fine shaped nose with flared nostrils. Her eyes were bright blue. Not too many eyelashes but those she had were mascarraed or perhaps dyed.

Dawn began to talk exclusively about herself, bringing in Patricia for light comedy. She talked with absolute confidence as if to a familiar audience. Nobody tried to halt the stream not even to say, 'Shall we take a look at the menu?' Eventually we did look at the chalk board above the bar but only when Dawn suggested it.

'Hey, I thought you were all hungry,' she said as if we'd been the ones doing the talking. Food was ordered. More wine for me and Jan, Dawn and Patricia were now sticking to water.

Dawn resumed her monologue. Patricia, usually such great company, sat turned towards her, enchanted by Dawn's ability to follow one sentence with yet another. Sometimes Patricia looked searchingly into our faces, giving us her huge, slow smile, like we must be having such fun listening to this tremendous, extraordinary woman she'd found.

Dawn talked about the new apartment she was buying. She was project managing the alterations and décor.

'Dawn's one helluva seamstress,' Patricia said proudly, 'She's made all the cushions.'

Dawn told us about the cushion material being a William Morris pattern that picked up the colour of the drapes and the painted book shelves. She said she was worried about Patricia's books because there were so many of them and they were all paper backs and very dog eared. Jan and I looked suitably worried on her behalf although both of us had too many dog eared paperbacks and were very fond of them. Dawn said Patricia's taste in art was 'absolute shit'. We nodded and laughed as if we knew and agreed. Patricia laughed and nodded too.

'She's right. My taste is shit. Dawn's going to teach me better taste.'

I tried to catch Jan's eye but she kept her gaze fixed on Dawn. Under the table I nudged her foot – she moved her foot away from mine. In my head I wondered if anyone would mind if I said, 'I'm just going outside for a breath of fresh air.' I'd hang around in the street doing some breathing and stretching exercises and then when everyone's attention had reverted to Dawn I'd slope off home. I wondered whether Jan might be thinking exactly the same thing and how amusing it would be if we both, by some synchronicity stood up and said, 'I'm just going outside for a breath of fresh air.'

'Am I missing the joke?' Dawn asked.

I realised I was smiling when obviously I should have been looking concerned about something she was saying. I was saved from replying because Jan did suddenly leap from her chair and rush outside. Before I could leap up and join her, Dawn was on her feet and through the door. Patricia grabbed my arm, 'Let Dawn handle this, Lucy.'

I sank back into my chair. 'Handle what?'

'I think Jan's pretty low at the moment.'

'How do you know?'

Patricia spread out her hands. 'Email. Jan writes me all the time.'

Dawn and Jan were coming back in, Dawn's arm around Jan's shoulders.

'I'm sorry,' Jan said wiping her eyes with the back of her hand. Dawn guided Jan to her chair as if she was incapable of making it unaided, then went to the bar and returned with another bottle of Still Water. She dropped a wad of paper napkins into Jan's lap and poured water into Jan's empty wine glass.

'This is what you need. Wine can be a real depressant.'

Jan sipped the water, tears still streaming down her face. The Dragon Bar was busier now with people coming in for their lunches, our table was the centre of furtive attention.

'I'm sorry,' Jan said again, 'You have no idea just how unhappy I am at the moment.'

I caught a reproachful glance from Patricia. Obviously as Jan's friend I should have had some idea. What could I say? Yes, I did know Jan was desperately unhappy but thought she'd prefer it if we kept off the subject and stuck to a mutual love of the home-grown vegetable?

Jan mopped tears with the napkins but they kept on coming. I fumbled for her hand but found myself squeezing her shoulder bag.

'Let her cry,' Dawn said, 'I've been there.'

Which was annoying as I'd have liked to have got in first with my own 'I've been there' not that it had occurred to me till Dawn said it. 'Me too,' I said but nobody seemed curious about any journey I'd made into the depth of despair. (I exaggerate). Dawn pulled her chair closer to Patricia's. She rested one hand on Patricia's thigh, the other she clasped around her glass of water. I noticed her jewellery; an impressive sapphire ring and a Snake's Eye gold band. I'd bet money that the Snake's Eye came from Patricia.

Dawn said, 'While Jan recovers can I share something about my husband Jefferson?' She fixed her gaze intently on my face. 'Lucy, the bastard frightens the living daylights out of me.'

Perhaps it was because I was on my fourth glass of wine and had hardly eaten anything what with all the listening and concentrating I'd been required to do, but I'd moved on in my thoughts from Snake's Eye to Garden Snakes and how they enjoyed lying in the sun to whether that made them susceptible to hawks which brought me back to Dawn, really and truly resembling a bird of prey but what bird? She was too diamond perfect to be an ornery buzzard but nevertheless with her sculpted features and way of sitting forward without allowing her shoulder blades to touch the back of her chair –.

Dawn frowned at me. 'Lucy, did you hear what I just said?'

Fortunately over many years I have perfected the ability to listen quite closely to a conversation while also day-dreaming. 'You said "the bastard frightens the living daylights out of me."' However my intonation was obviously faulty because she looked queryingly at Patricia.

'It's ok Dawn. That's just Lucy's way. She often looks distracted but she's one hundred percent on the ball. Am I right Luce?'

I nodded and tried to look 'one hundred percent on the ball'. Dawn leant back in her seat and began. 'As Patricia's probably told you, I have two lovely daughters. I love my kids. Hurt them, you hurt me. He wrote them a letter—,'

At the tables around us I was aware that the conversations had slowed and quietened – Dawn's gaze flickered around the room as if ensuring she had an attentive audience.

'—in it he said,' she paused, took a sip of water, 'that Patricia was giving it to me . . . up the arse. Can you imagine how that made me feel, Lucy?'

I experienced an overwhelming, inappropriate desire to laugh which I knew would be a disastrous response. I picked up a spare serviette and blew my nose heartily while surreptitiously sucking on the bottom section. I took my time scrunching the serviette into a ball and tucking it into my sleeve.

'How old are your daughters?' I asked.

She turned her killer blue eyes on me. 'That's immaterial.'

'Yes,' Patricia agreed, 'That is *really* immaterial. The fact is that true or false – he wrote that in a letter to his own children. Jefferson is so gross.'

'He does sound awful,' Jan said. Her tears had stopped.

'An understatement, Jan,' Patricia replied but not reprovingly like she'd sounded with me.

'I just wanted to share that with you both. You in particular Jan, so you know that I feel your pain.'

Jan flapped her hands apologetically. 'Honestly Dawn, I've got nothing to complain about that doesn't happen to someone somewhere every day; a girlfriend gets a new girlfriend – wants to move her in and,' she gulped, 'me out. I'll have to live with mum which means that I'll end up being her carer, which means I'll have to give up my job which is no sort of a job really but it suited me.'

Patricia laid her hand on Jan's shoulder and squeezed, 'You're having a tough time.'

'No, no. Nothing as bad as Dawn and her husband.'

'Ex-husband any day now, the bastard.'

Soon afterwards the party broke up. We stood outside on the pavement to say our goodbyes. Dawn gripped Jan's elbows, 'You visit us the next time you're in New York.'

'I'll do that,' Jan said as if she were the jet-setting type.

I sensed a coolness towards me coming from Dawn and Patricia. Somehow I knew I wouldn't be asked to visit them in New York and I wasn't. A cool kiss on the cheek from Dawn, an arm squeeze from Patricia but combined with a look of puzzlement in her eyes as if I'd proved a disappointment.

I watched them stroll away, just their fingertips linked. At 'Soak', the new luxury bath product shop they paused and peered in the window. I wasn't surprised, Dawn was definitely a luxury bath product person and soon Patricia might become one as well. I turned to share this insight with Jan as she emerged from the Dragon Bar, her two spare fleeces over her arm.

'I left them behind.' She gave me a watery smile, 'Well, wasn't that nice?'

I said, 'Actually Jan it wasn't nice at all. Dawn is totally self-absorbed. She'll suck all the life and exuberance out of Patricia and eventually dump her for a fresher, wealthier model. I give them two years.'

For the first time ever I saw Jan angry, her eyes hot and fierce, her breathing coming in quick, loud gasps.

'*You* give them two years?'

'Okay, five years. Certainly not forever. I'd say a limited time-line.'

Jan's eyes, eyebrows, nose and mouth configured into one huge sneer, 'And what do *we* have to put next to their two years? Next to their 'limited time-line'?'

'Steady on Jan.'

'Two years of getting older on my own, looking after my mother, trying to avoid bumping into Eileen and her new girlfriend walking their dogs on the West Hill—'

'That's how you feel now but I promise a moment will come when you start looking forward again.'

'Looking forward?' Jan shouted, 'Dawn and Patricia will have more to look forward to than exchanging courgette seedlings for runner beans.'

'Cannellino beans. Well I'm sorry you don't find our exchange of seedlings very thrilling, I foolishly imagined it might be fun.'

'I'm in love with Patricia,' she spat out.

'With Patricia?' I echoed.

I felt like a small rodent in a box of sand searching for an appropriate sentence, certain I'd left a juicy one somewhere containing the elements of 'immoderate crying when apparently in love with someone else, Eileen, Bedlington Terriers, lack of trust combined with secretive and underhand behaviour'. My day was dissolving into a row of opened cans of worms.

'Don't worry Lucy, I don't intend to dump any of this on you, I just wanted to say the words to someone.'

I wound my way through the steep lanes and alleys that take me up onto the West Hill. I found a bench that looked out over the sea. The sea sparkled. The sun was about two inches above the horizon. I imagined Patricia and Dawn on the train, their shoulders touching, both wearing their expensive sun glasses even though the light was fading. Dawn was possibly thinking, 'Hmm, that went off pretty well now I don't need to meet Pat's English friends for at least another five years, if ever.'

Lucky Patricia. Was I in love with her as well? I was certainly fond of her but at that moment a little less fond to coincide with her obviously feeling a little less fond of me. I'd never have the courage to fall for a woman like Dawn but was I perhaps in love with Jan? No, although for several years I'd nurtured a soft spot for Eileen. Perhaps I should consider buying a dog but not a Bedlington Terrier or a Labrador.

Was I a tiny bit in love with myself? Now that was a possibility. I'd always felt encouraged by the line from the Whitney Houston song about 'learning to love yourself being the greatest love of all'.

Back on the London train I visualised Patricia taking Dawn's hand. 'I'm so sorry about Lucy. She's changed. I'm thinking about deleting her from my round-robin mailing list.'

'She seems a little weird but don't do anything on my account.'

Patricia twists the Snake's Eye ring that cost her a week's money. 'You were just wonderful. The way you took care of Jan. I so appreciate it.'

'Honey, it was nothing,' Dawn says.

They kiss. The dark lenses of their sun glasses tap against each other as the train speeds into a tunnel.

NEVER CAN SAY GOODBYE

NEVER CAN SAY GOODBYE

KAREN MCLEOD

The last day of my marriage, my wife, Lorna and I were on honeymoon in Barbados.

She had paid the six thousand pounds for two weeks all inclusive at Turtle Egg Paradise Resort and my contribution was a poem entitled, *the sea food buffet will run forever.*

I met Lorna the night my long term girlfriend Suzie had stopped taking her lithium and set the garden shed on fire. Lorna had arrived in her uniform and helmet, jumping out the fire engine with her unusual face. She introduced herself quickly as Firefighter Trout. At first, she struck me as unattractive with her tiny eyes and big face. The helmet hid all her hair and the tight chin strap was squeezing her double chin. But within moments she'd unrolled then controlled the powerful jet of water coming out the hose and stamped out the last of the fire into the dandelions with her sooty boots. Her strange face became replaced with a fuzzy heroism.

I had watched the dramatic scene from the patio, making mental notes for future poems. All published writers say, *everything is material and nothing is ever wasted.* The smoking floor where my writing desk had stood, along with the stack of eight unfinished poetry collections, was now charcoal, proving that all material can be wasted. I had cried for all the lost similes that had gone up in smoke. Lorna came over and told me a cheering-up story. She described that before my emergency, she'd put out a fire above the bookies along the high street. Some woman had been drying her underwear in the microwave and it had caught aflame. Only two warped wires of the bra remained. I should have realised then, it was one of those omens from the cosmos; Lorna was telling me that she dampened down women's underwear for a living. She put out the flames, not ignited them.

Still, this was life and in order to make art, I had to take from what was presented to me. I made the fire crew an instant coffee and they all enjoyed one of my scones around the kitchen table. After my main fuse box had been tested, Lorna got out a safety check book and asked if I had a bedroom routine. I said *I did thank you very much,* a little bit shocked - I told her I brushed my teeth and made sure the dog flap was locked. She laughed her small eyes closed and said she meant did I check my escape route before going to bed? Apparently, in the world of fire safety, it should be clear of obstacles. She said keys should be where they are supposed to be for an easy escape, in case of fire. I said I was too creative to have a set routine for keys.

In case of fire soon became one of our coupley jokes. Not really a joke, more a non-joke, an amusing bridge of words between us. *Don't kiss each other in Bromley High Street, in case of fire!* that sort of thing, which was only entertaining to the two of us and not really my humour. I know it was just a term of endearment we used to keep us safely attached to one another.

Because Lorna was into competitive sports she'd made sure we got the first slot down the registry office the day civil partnerships became legal. It had seemed like the right thing to do at the time. I hoped it was love, I suspected it was because I ached for her when she left the room and felt sick when she came back in. All my friends said it was too soon and that I should think about *my actions* more. My friends did everything slowly, as if they could control consequence, as if they had a forever to live in. I was already in my mid-thirties and still an unpublished poet with a part-time job in Boots in The Glades. I knew life was going on somewhere without me, so I had decided that I shouldn't ignore any adventure offered to me and grab it with both hands. After dating Lorna for three months she had got down on one knee and proposed outside Pizza Express. *Why not* I had thought and said *yes, get up, people are looking*. I hadn't had one wife yet, and I knew from history if you were going to be a proper Bohemian artist and have mistresses you needed to get a wife first.

A photographer from the Bromley Shopper shouted *cheese!* as we stood on the steps of the town hall under an arch made by the firefighter's axes. It was very exciting, all the commotion. Lorna's mother, Brenda, had come up from Eastbourne for the occasion. She appeared like a character straight out a Beryl Cook painting, round bottomed and tipping over drunk. She showered us with biodegradable confetti horseshoes. Later, after the champagne, gin and tequila chasers, Brenda slipped off her hat from her tight curled hair and grabbed my hand. She said how beautiful we, meaning me and Lorna, both looked in our matching flame retardant outfits. And as the three of us travelled along in the limousine towards Brighton, where we were staying for a night before the honeymoon, Brenda grasped my fingers and said, *you're one of us now, you're a Trou*t.

My parents had decided to take a Saga mini coach break, destination Cadbury's World in Birmingham, to escape what my mother called *all the nonsense*. I didn't mind and even if I had I wouldn't say as I'm not one to make a fuss. I still have the page from the newspaper for them in a gold frame, should they want to see it. It says in capitals LESBIANS SAY I DO!!!

It's the three exclamation marks after the words which I stare at and not how Lorna is there in the picture, all real with a proud grin. The newspaper received twenty three letters of complaint, mainly from the Bickley and West Wickham area. They printed a selection - to 'give both sides of the story' - which was made up of the words like: unnatural, God, corrupting children, filthy, not in my day and animal cruelty. The animal cruelty bit must be because in the photo Lorna is holding her overweight cat, Morris, who is squeezed into a page boy's outfit.

We flew out of Gatwick after staying the one night. Her mother, Brenda, had insisted on booking a room so she could enjoy every last second with us. Brenda and me got drunk on house white wine and Lorna sat watching drinking iced tap water. The more I drank the more I started to feel I should have married Lorna's mother. But as soon as I'd thought it, Lorna took her mother upstairs to bed. It was as if she had heard my thoughts. By the time she got back to our honeymoon suite, she told me I was flat out on the bed face down in an unromantic position.

As the plane thumped down Lorna leant over and whispered, *I feel like we are finally, you know, cemented as a couple.* She had tried to hug me though we were restricted by our seat belts so had ended up kissing my ear. I tried hard not to imagine a newly surfaced patio with my body stuck underneath it. I began to worry how many hours there were in two weeks. We'd only ever been on a long weekend in Devon and it wasn't the smoothest of breaks as I had been mistaken for her daughter, twice.

In Barbados, a woman in smart tan shorts and a crisp blue blouse greeted us out the front of Turtle Egg Paradise. She was stood on the marble steps which were a brilliant white in the sunshine. Her skin shone beautifully like the best quality milk chocolate. On her name badge was

Barbara and I thought what an odd name for her as she didn't look like a Barbara. Anyhow, Barbara was holding a tray of free tropical punch. I drank my rum punch too quickly and so felt like having a holiday cigarette but Lorna's voice came straight into my head saying, *forty percent of deaths in the home are because of cigarettes, cigars or pipes.*

In the reception area we waited in line behind all the other couples for the check in desk. I noticed we were the only couple made up of two females, but didn't say anything as it was not a unique observation. Lorna was holding the travel pouch and I fanned myself with my passport, looking across at the bridge crossing over two out of the five deluxe swimming pools. I wandered over to a small patch of garden. Sat on the branch of a frangipane tree was a green parrot, its hard tongue hovering in and out of its beak as if it were deciding whether to speak. Up on a balcony I noticed a man looking down through a pair of binoculars at where I was standing, or maybe he was bird watching. As I shaded my eyes to the sun he swung the binoculars from his face and said something to a woman in a towel.

By the time we got to rest our elbows on the cool marble of the reception, I'd had another glass of punch and given Lorna an accidental kiss on her diver's watch. I'd gone for her hand but missed it, catching my lip on her new bulky purchase from the airport. The receptionist stared at the two of us, a swift study from my face across to hers. I let go of her fingers, realising it wasn't done here. Then the receptionist asked the question. *Would you prefer twin beds Miss Trout?* And Lorna snapped *no, we would not like twin beds but would like a big king size bed,* in a voice which made the receptionist tap quickly on his keyboard and not look up from his fingers. I was going to add to do it to each other in but I realised it was the holiday punch making me verbally loose.

That first night Lorna arrived late for dinner as she had gone to book her shark dive for day four of the honeymoon and been haggling over the price, not that she couldn't afford it. When she sat down I remarked how white and ill we both looked compared to the staff and other holiday makers. We'd dressed up for dinner - me in white shirt and loose trousers, but with sparkly flip flops and Lorna in Bermuda shorts and an open collared Hawaiian shirt, though I had tried to get her to wear something more feminine. Barbara had shown us to our table in the corner under the stairs by what turned out to be the door leading to the kitchen. At first I told myself this spot in the restaurant was the most romantic, as we needed several candles to see what we were doing. Every so often the door would open and a different waiter with a big toothy smile would appear with plates running up his arm. Lorna couldn't see as she had her back to the door, but on more than one occasion, one of the kitchen staff's black faces would appear at the round window set in the door and stare over at us.

Lorna had remarked, *they are having a good laugh in the kitchen aren't they. Nice to hear staff happy in their work, they probably aren't unionised you know*. I didn't like to say the obvious, about how they were probably laughing at us, looking like the odd couple, so I filled up my glass with expensive French wine. I felt uncomfortable as Lorna gave me a slow kiss over my seafood platter (she had a vegetarian kebab) and I took my lips away quickly, aware that the waitress was watching.

The waitress didn't return to clear away the empty shell of my lobster for twenty minutes. Lorna began to look around with that look on her face like when she had shouted at the sofa salesman and we were asked to leave the building. I knew the kiss had resulted in our plates not being cleared away, but then I try not to take things personally. All my friends said to us at home how people were laid back in the Caribbean and that they took their own time to do things in. *Abroad time,* my mother calls it. But this wasn't *abroad time.* In the end when Lorna went to the toilet I put the plates behind a giant terracotta plant pot and helped myself to the next course.

Later on, after the calypso steel drum band, we sat on the veranda in our complimentary dressing gowns enjoying the heat of the evening on our bare legs. A book of Sylvia Plath's poetry was unopened on the table. Lorna was drinking her fourth pina colada and telling me stories of sea cucumbers and nurse sharks and the behaviour of anchovies - how they swirl together into one massive giant shoal when a shark is near. At one point, as I quietly removed watermelon pips from a plate of complimentary fruit, I just gazed out of focus at her and watched her lips move. I had a secret fantasy about Suzie turning up and setting the beach huts on fire. I watched her lips open and close with accounts of the coral reef. It was more interesting when she told me the fire stories. When she did her impersonation of a shark, flashing her canine teeth towards me, and then began kissing me, all the way from my clavicle up to behind my ear, a thought crossed my mind.

I could do quite nicely without you.

I gulped down my drink as I realised I had thought it. The love had been tested and found out to have faulty wiring. It was startling. A whole week hadn't yet passed since the wedding. Another thought cut into my mind. It was one of those thoughts you shouldn't admit you have.

I hope she gets eaten by a shark.

It would solve everything. I would be able to play the part of the grieving widow and Brenda her mother would come and stay and we both could mourn and drink in Lorna's garden on the patio. I could take up smoking again. I could find someone who really appreciates the poetic form and doesn't just listen and clap everything I do, like Lorna did. I would be free to leave candles burning wax on a television if I wanted to.

The morning of the shark dive, I had a fresh fruit salad with kiwi and a big jug of fresh coffee. Barbara was beginning to warm up and give us a faint smile of recognition at breakfast. She brought me my cranberry juice without me having to ask for it and she had stopped calling Lorna *sir*. Lorna had wrapped up a croissant in a serviette and secreted it into her rucksack to eat on the coach.

Before Lorna went she handed me her itinerary for the day, swimming with dolphins at twelve, followed by the shark cage dive at four. She kissed me and said I love you like she knew that everything was different. She had repeated it so many times it had worn thin. The less I felt it, the more she said it.

I waved her off onto the mini bus and returned to our room to place my wedding band in the safe and get out some cash. For a little while I could be who I was without her. I chose to go to a public beach where no honeymoon couples would be rubbing oil into each other's creases. I found the whole happiness business nauseating. The couples gave off this predetermined cosy air, with their daily positions on the same sun loungers. As if Lorna agreed with their settings, she had begun to speak about us moving into a larger house, upgrading the TV set into a cinema surround sound package and where we should go on holiday next year. She spoke about property with a desperate tone of desire as if it would save our lives. In her mind the houses should just get bigger and more expensive as we climbed the property ladder. She suggested I sell my one bedroom garden flat and we consolidate our assets and get a joint pension fund and a cash ISA. She said we should save for an IVF fund as I was the one with years of menstrual freedom ahead of me.

I tied a sarong around my chest, picked up my straw beach bag and took the water taxi to a public beach across the other side of the island. There was a small shack of a bar where I ordered a beer. On a stool I let my flip flops drop off and dug holes with my toes in the cold shaded sand. I took out my notebook and wrote the date at the top of the page. Chalked up on the board was a menu of the catch of the day. I noticed under *tiger prawns* were the words *Mahi Mahi.* The bar man described it, in his lovely thick Caribbean accent, as being a dolphin fish. I thought of Lorna straight away. It was about now she would be frolicking about with the shiny nosed dolphins. I ordered Mahi Mahi with a side of coleslaw and chips. Then I ordered another beer and squeezed fresh lime over the meat. It was the juiciest fish I had ever tasted. In the late afternoon, I paid a local woman to rub aloe vera into my burnt thighs and ordered beers for everyone at the bar. As the orange sun sank into the line of sea, I danced to reggae with the bar man and his friends and smoked a whole joint which made me feel like there were parrots in every tree watching me.

I had expected to find Lorna full of dive talk sitting on the balcony of our room when I had returned. The room was as I had left it. I sat on the balcony writing a postcard to Brenda from us, settling my paranoia with a large gin. Across the hotel on the opposite balcony I saw that man again, looking at me through his binoculars. I took a large swig of duty free gin and stuck my fingers up at him. He stopped looking and talked to his wife. I ate at the buffet alone stuffing my face with deep fried chilli prawns, mini cheeseburgers and onion rings.

When the phone rang at ten o'clock I presumed it would be Lorna. A man's voice said that I should get to the hospital as there had been a terrible accident and they would send a car to fetch me immediately. They said I should prepare myself. I swigged some gin and got dressed in a tizzy.

I turned up at the hospital relieved to find the hospital looked less serious than our British ones because of the palm trees and white washed steps. I was shown to a small air-conditioned room which had two chairs and a low table with a box of tissues on it. A woman came and sat with me, explaining the dive had gone wrong and the cage had somehow opened, as there was a lack of dolphin fish lately the sharks were hungry and had become unusually vicious.

She showed me into a cold room with metal trolleys lined up in it. She said I had to identify my friend Miss Lorna Trout, delicately asking me if I had access to her insurance documents. There was a trolley with a long white sheet over it and I remembered thinking I was about to look at a dead animal as the bulge under the sheet was too small to be Lorna's wide body. When they turned back the sheet there was just an arm, severed at the shoulder. I had to say that the arm was Lorna's, because I recognised the wedding ring on her finger; it was the same ring as mine back in the hotel room safe. I would know that hand anywhere I remember saying. I thought the way the blue tipped fingers were curled into themselves was cupped into a small wave.

In the taxi back to the hotel I asked myself the question, *how much do my thoughts weigh?*

I sat on the balcony and watched the man on the balcony watch me through his binoculars. I drank all the gin and went down to the beach in my towelling dressing gown. The singer on the terrace was singing an Andrew Lloyd Webber medley. I threw Sylvia Plath's *Ariel* into the sea, hoping a shark would swallow the poetry.

THE PIANIST'S HANDS

THE PIANIST'S HANDS

SOPHIA BLACKWELL

The night of the day Jess left, the house was quieter than it had ever been. I couldn't stop thinking about how she'd looked that morning, surrounded by all her worldly goods in the back seat. They didn't seem like much, not even for eighteen years on earth. Her face was pinched and white, nose-stud and lip-ring glittering in sharp relief. For two years, it had just been us, and I was wondering what I'd do without her. I wasn't all that worried about how she'd cope without me. She seemed to have done brilliantly so far.

I sat at the kitchen table, my first cigarette in ten years burning in a saucer at my side, a drink from one of Jonathan's old sticky-labelled bottles beside it, and an unopened letter in front of me. I'd hurriedly scooped it into my pocket that morning, in the rush to get my daughter out of the door and into adulthood. I'd kept it with me all the horrendous morning, warm against my thigh like a hand. I'd recognised the handwriting and hoped it would give me some comfort later- not that the writer was ever big on comfort.

The last letter I'd got had made me do something foolish and irreversible. It said, 'Talia, I've got something to tell you. But I want to know that I'm yours first. Prove it however you want.' I'd done it, and sent the photograph; now I was waiting for the answer.

I'd cried all the way home. Jonathan was sweeter than he'd been in years. 'Do you want anything?' he asked. 'Talia? Come on, whatever you want. A triple Jack and Coke? An ounce of Red Leb?'

That was what we smoked a hundred years ago; a softer high then the dope I've smelled in my daughter's hair, on her curtains, in the bathroom before she goes out on the town. I don't know what my ex-husband, with his new driving glasses, was doing offering me drugs. He's getting paunchy – that girl of his must feed him well – and his hairline's finally starting to recede. I used to love running my fingers through his nest of dark curls; my beautiful, bedsit-dwelling, poetry-spouting boy with his clarinet and his second-hand cat. Now here we are, messily divorced instead of messily married, Jon with his olive-eyed girlfriend and me with my grey hairs and ghosts- and my new tattoo. Nice middle-aged women don't get tattoos, and if they do, they don't let their impressionable, scarred and already multi-pierced teenage daughters see them.

I'd been in the kitchen, bending to get the juice out of the fridge. She moves so silently these days. I heard her shout, 'Mum!' and turned around like she'd scalded herself- you never lose that reflex, even when you're about to lose your kids.

She was still so beautiful it stopped my breath, even with the metal and the mauve-tinged hair. She'd had that effect on me since they dropped her into my arms, limp as an empty glove. She got my hair, bless her- uncontrollable wads of brown lint, now a greyish purple. I used to have that body- endless legs, jutting hipbones, skin like blue-tinged milk where mine's wrinkled and slack, knots of muscle and veins fighting to the surface. There are many marks on this nearly-forty body, but I'd only chosen one of them and she was staring right at it.

'What the hell is that?' she said, as well she might.

'It's a tattoo, Jess.' I was going to swig out of the carton but I'm always telling her not to do that. I can stop now, I suppose. I got a glass.

'But you're . . . you can't do that, Mum! I mean, where'd you, like, get it?'

'Somewhere in Camden. Quite nice, actually. Sort of girlie. Clean, anyway.' Camden's her patch now. She goes after school, rolling up her skirt with one hand and a spliff with the other. 'Don't tell your Dad,' I said, cravenly. 'He'll only think I'm having a mid-life crisis too.'

'Are you?' She doesn't trust either of us these days.

'No, baby. I'm not. Now come here and give your mad mother a hug.'

Mad? Apart from the encroaching empty-nest syndrome, I'd never been saner. But as we embraced I could feel the sharply edged lines flaring at my back, the new heat in my blood rushing towards the ink, like whatever was inside me couldn't wait to meet it.

I got up from the table like the creaky old woman I'd become when I wasn't paying attention, and poured myself another whisky before going back to the envelope. I was listening to my old music, a raw-edged jazz that people write essays about now but hardly ever play.

I turned the envelope over. I knew it was from Tyler; my old accompanist, my friend, my lover, who I hadn't seen in person in eighteen years of postcards and afternoons combing record stores for liner notes that said 'Piano: Tyler Corrigan.' Two last names- they tend to do that, Americans. Old money, and even in third-hand suits, Tyler Corrigan looked it, sharp as hell in a lacquer-black suit, polished brogues and a snappy necktie.

Those hands were the only giveaway. When they were naked, without their bulky leather gloves, they spoke volumes to strangers. I preferred the way they spoke to the piano, to my skin. I was a jazz singer; I tell people at parties, in bars. Jonathan, who was in the band too, doesn't feel the need to. He's got his business, his other life, but I couldn't make it through an evening without it pouring out of my mouth, hot and delicious as held-in smoke. Not to Jess, though. She didn't need to know I was a jazzer. It sounds dirty, and from what I remember, it was. The bass thrum, the hustle and flow around us, the wall of the brass; all of it was sex.

When that rapper Jess liked, before her Goth phase – Lil' Daddy Jones or something- sampled one of our riffs, it was so hard not to tell her. For a couple of hours, we could have been cool again. We were in the car with Jonathan, Jess tapping her fingers in the back, and there it was, adorning some booty-shaking bitch-filled track. Even though we knew our days were numbered, my eyes met his and we smiled, tight-lipped, remembering together.

Our singer, Bertha Lee, was a third-rate diva, a black, barrel-shaped powerhouse, bridal trails of sequins streaking behind her in the dark. Every night she'd sweep in, arms above her head, holding us all in a hot, sweaty, light-spattered embrace that had even the hardened cynics crowding to the front, wanting to get heckled to see if she remembered their names.

The first night Tyler and I went home together, Bertha was wearing white, accessorised with a yellowed fur stole so big it looked like she'd clubbed a polar bear on the way to the spotlight. When she went for a bathroom break and a little adoration from the crowd, she'd murmur grudgingly, 'My backing singer, Talia Feldman …' and I got to sing some of the hokey old standards I loved.

Tyler's playing felt like hands on my shoulders, holding me up, warm and intimate as a dance partner. My voice and Tyler's fingers slow-danced until Bertha appeared in front of me. I knew it was time to get off the stage, get myself a drink, and my own little helping of praise – not enough, never enough.

I sat in the dark, pulsing with slowly calming nerves and a longing I couldn't name. Naked without the pianist's hands, I let the night wash over me, run its smoke-scented fingers through my hair.

In the break, Tyler came over, all flushed cheeks. 'Hey, Talia! Girl, you were storming tonight. Course, you always are, but …'

'Yeah, you were too, especially on the Cole Porter stuff.'

'You know my favourites, don't you?' Those hands landed on the back of my chair, as though about to rock me- or push me. 'Why don't you sing something now?'

'Oh, baby, I'm done singing.'

'For them, you're done.' The crowd was starting to look like some hellish modernist painting, all blurred edges and yawning mouths. 'Not for me.'

As I sang softly, I started to feel tentative, little-boy tugs on my hair, as though trying to pull it straight strand by strand. As Tyler started to stroke my neck through my layers of hair, I picked it up and lifted it out of the way like a soft, heavy curtain, asking for that touch there. I knew Tyler could feel the vibrations in my throat, so that even in the din and darkness, the music stayed.

On the way out, we stopped to pick up our wages from Jonathan, who was the only one the band-leaders would trust with money. Tyler strode out of the door and up the stairs ahead of me, muttering about a cigarette. I heard the click and purr of the lighter, saw in the doorway a dull gold paper flare like a lantern guttering out.

Jonathan looked up the stairs after Tyler. We were just friends then, him and me, though sometimes we ended up in bed. The love we made was far from perfect, but it was so sweet we always felt like we were getting away with something.

'You be careful,' he said, no edge to his voice. 'No disrespect to you or Tyler, but that girl's trouble. No one knows where she's been.'

Tyler shared her bedroom with her piano. No one else we knew had one. We travelled light, leaving at midnight to avoid the rent and questions about why the walls were now purple. I could tell it worried her, how much she loved that thing; you couldn't run away with a piano on your back, and something that size would be even harder to hide than love.

Tyler reached for my hand. While she was only a little shorter than me, and I was a tall girl – still am, of course – my hand was almost twice the size of hers. I wondered how those child's hands could be so gymnastic on the keys, especially as the left one didn't look quite right – the thumb and one finger seemed a little skewed, like they'd been broken and not properly set.

Without her chunky watch, jacket and waistcoat, her body was unmistakably female, hips heavier than mine. She took off her shirt like her father might have done after a hard day, wrenching off the tie at her throat as though she didn't love it and pacing the room in her undershirt to open the window, like a matinee bad-boy in a white wife-beater undershirt that clung to the bound curves of her chest. I was careful to look at the parts of her I knew- cheekbones sharpened by hard living, the sinews bunched at her wrists, the fine skin on the back of her neck, shaved clean as soap.

She unzipped my black dress. There was something over-practised in that nonchalance of hers that I found endearing. I looked down at the bleached keyboard of my ribs, my tatty ivory bra, feeling like she was the magician with her sharp lapels and silk hankies, and I was the assistant, or the dumbstruck crowd.

When she laid me down, my legs chalk-white against her dark pinstripes, I knew this would be different from all the sex I'd ever had so far- not like wrestling, or play-fighting, or running in heels. This would be like dancing.

Everyone has dreams. Mine was to be an actress, but there's only so many times you can stand alone under lights hearing, 'Thank you,' from the dark. Tyler, while she was great at what she did, wanted to be a concert pianist, like her father. She called him The Maestro, at first ironically, then less so, as she started to want what he had. A dirt-poor scholarship boy, he'd had the touch of genius as well as the hard graft that got him a conservatory education; she'd had the training too, though her father had never approved. He'd never approved of how good she looked in his suits either.

The Maestro was who she got her gloss from, that aristocratic attitude slung over her shoulders like one of Bertha's furs, that had people opening doors, 'There you go, Sir.' The Maestro had the kind of connections you couldn't laugh at, numbers and favours owed, an intricate network that meant more to him than money or success; it was the power he could wield that mattered. In that way, Tyler was exactly like him.

After an awkward lunch while he was playing in London, Tyler and her father struck a deal. If she'd come back to America, go into his music copyright business with him; if she stopped playing around with blues-men and chorus girls, he'd give her a platform to prove herself at the Godin Hall. It was a great place, a retro palace of gin and gas-lamps, long gone now.

The piece she chose was Lizst's 'Transcendental Etudes' and even with my limited knowledge, I knew it was diabolical – particularly for someone with such small hands. At the piano, pouring with sweat, her usually bone-cool face flushed and clenched, Tyler looked like someone trying to escape from Hell.

It's shameful, but I didn't want her to succeed that night; not just because it meant losing her, but because I wanted this out of her system. I didn't like who she was when that demon was in her; she became like her father; a scowler, a slammer, an artist of silences.

Maybe it would have all been different if I'd told her I loved her. There were times when it felt like I did; when I watched her strutting to her spot on the stage and settling behind the keyboard with a flourish, or rooting in a drawer for the right necktie to go with her suit, how her brow furrowed like a little boy's when she fastened her watch round her wrist, the way she'd stand and rub her nose when she'd forgotten something.

Sometimes I imagined a future for us. I'd wake to the sound of her husky voice; I'd sleep in her bad-boy undershirts and breathe her scent of tobacco and hair-lacquer. I'd taste the sea-salt sweat of hard work at the piano, the sediment on her skin a delicious shock to my tongue as I dipped my mouth to the open clef of her wrist.

One night, the fingers on her right hand hurt so much that she had to stop playing. In the unexpected silence, we lay on the mattress and she told me about her fingers. Once, in the middle of an argument, her father had grabbed her hand, twisted and forgotten to stop until it was too late. In the emergency room, he'd bought Tyler her first cup of coffee. He'd forgotten, that was how she put it – a moment too long, but one she had to live with, no matter how good she got.

As the summer wore on I spent more time with Jonathan- sweet, easy, uncomplicated Jon. The sex was still clumsy but at least it was safe; sometimes, struggling under Tyler's weight, I could see she wasn't with me any more. Her mind was going through the motions. I could almost see it working, glittering harshly like the exposed hammers of a piano under lights.

We were all there for her big night, suitably overdressed. Jonathan was smart in a schoolboy suit, Bertha dripping in rhinestones, and me in a copper-coloured flapper dress, a rusty velvet flower behind one ear. We sat in the front row, so Tyler could see us.

Just as the lights went down, we were joined by a new, hustling group- loud, awkward, all elbows and feet and theatrically shushed laughter, deeply drunk. Bertha stopped fussing. Jonathan fell silent. You know their kind when you're in show business. Even if you're only the backing singer for a bargain-basement Billie Holiday – if you can't recognise arseholes, you have no business even doing that.

There were only three of them, though they made enough noise for an army- a shiny, hard-faced little blonde and a haughty black woman with a loudhailer voice, clinging to a fat man who looked like a dyspeptic clown. They behaved as though they had far better places to be- and inwardly I begged them to go and find these places before Tyler played. When anyone else was on, they could do what the hell they wanted – laugh, chat, set fire to the place. I'd help.

My darling strode onto the stage, her face grim; she didn't see me. I suppose it was too dark. She sat down and took off her jacket, accompanied by a ripple of applause so polite that it seemed to suck the oxygen out of the room.

She picked her way over the keys, hands flying up and back towards her body as though trying to demonstrate her restraint, while the sticking-up cowlick at the back of her head, flopping up and down, betrayed her need. Her hands moved like a wildly dancing couple, swinging apart and drawn back together, mirroring each other.

Just for a second, I lost myself. I saw what she was trying to do and I embraced it.

The nasty little blonde muttered something in the clown's ear and he laughed. I heard them muttering. 'I know,' said the other woman loudly.

I didn't see Tyler falter once, but I knew she heard- I saw the stiffness in her shoulders, where there had been fluid movement a moment ago. Those sculpted cheekbones were shining with drops of sweat, overlaying each other like drips of wax as her fingers moved, faster and faster as though the keyboard was something else she was trying to break free from.

Her shirt. Her shirt was sticking to her body with sweat. She hadn't bound her breasts- she didn't, when she played. She needed to move freely. I could feel confusion hissing around us. We steeled ourselves, Bertha's eyes half-lidded, Jonathan leaning fervently forward. We were ready to protect our own.

I heard a barely suppressed gust of laughter from the blonde. She whispered into the ear of the fat clown, who finally woke up and bellowed, 'Fucking hell, that's not a guy!'

Around us the audience whispered and shifted in their seats, like this was somehow Tyler's fault.

'Honestly…' the black woman murmured, and the blonde cackled, 'No… no, it's a girl! Look!'

A girl? She'd been a little Tyler, yes, a person. Never a girl.

I shot the blonde an evil look, which she ignored. Her powdered face looked blank in the half-light. In our clubs, we would have mocked them while the band wailed behind us, but here, we failed. I failed.

In the chaos of the climax, some of the steel that Tyler had been forging into her bones came to the surface and shone. Her touch got some of its finesse back, like when she made love to me; packing all that fire and longing into something gentle. In that last ragged minute, she did what she'd come to do.

Shame no one noticed but us. They were all staring at her breasts, scanning her face for feminine softness. During another round of even less impressed applause – as though they were punishing her for deceiving them- I watched her reach for a white handkerchief and press it to her dripping face, wiping herself away.

There are thousands of small ways to fail someone; the unsent letter, the third cancelled date, the moment when Tyler came up to me after the concert and I couldn't meet her eyes. I wondered about it all the way home on the bus; if I'd jumped in and defended her, would I have redeemed myself, or made it worse? Still, there were other opportunities I'd missed; I should have admitted it hadn't been perfect, promised her there would be other times.

When we got home that night, every impatient twitch and sigh of hers made it worse; I wanted her to shout and throw things, but she got angry like her father did- silently, choking me slowly.

'You shouldn't let it stop you,' I blurted, too faintly, too late. 'Don't give up your dreams.'

'Really?' Her voice had lost its Southern warmth; its slowness seemed a form of torture. 'I didn't think you cared much for them.'

'I do ... I think you're amazing.'

'What do you dream about, Talia?' She was tapping out a tune on the coffee-table, a series of muted clacks. 'Do you dream about anything? Do you want anything? Or do you just want to drink and screw and sing those corny old songs until you're a hundred years old?'

'Doesn't sound too bad.'

'For Christ's sake, it is ... We can't live like this forever, girl. We're getting too old to wait tables and live in these little rooms and fuck anything that moves.' She was rolling herself a cigarette, fumbling stiff-fingered for her tobacco. 'Don't think I don't know what you're doing with that boy, either.'

'I never said I wasn't.'

'You never say anything, you never do anything ... Christ!' Her hand smacked down on the table. 'It's not even like ... that boy's nothing, he's nothing like me, he's just a little dreamer like you. And I don't know if you've noticed, even though God knows everyone else has, but he's a boy and I- through no fault of my own, I might add – am a fucking girl. So what the hell does that make you?'

'You're asking me what I am? Have you looked at yourself lately?'

'Hell, all I do is look at myself. I look at myself and I don't ... ' she took a deep drag from her cigarette. 'I don't see anyone I know.'

We didn't say much more after that. The smell of her cigarette followed me out.

Tyler was right about one thing, anyway; the party was over. When her father had a stroke, she went back to America as planned, like our time together was no more than a Grand Tour for The Maestro's child, whose name he'd never changed when she turned out to be a girl.

By the time he finally died, more silent and angry than ever, the band had broken up. It didn't all go to hell at once; we had smaller gigs, missed rehearsals, new line-ups, rifts and revisions before we called it a day. Sometimes it's harder if something isn't a total disaster – faint hope can be worse than outright failure.

I couldn't keep going, anyway – not with the seams of my gowns splitting mid-song and Bertha giving me knowing looks as I staggered off the smoky stage to puke in the dressing-room sink. At least we were a handsome couple, and it was a hell of a party, Jonathan grinning in his new suit and me in an off-the-shoulder gown with one of my Lady Day white corsages at the hip. We sent Tyler an invitation to the wedding, knowing it would arrive too late; another small way to fail someone.

The night of the day Jess left, I read Tyler's letter, which I was hoping would be a consolation. It wasn't. It punched the base out of my beaten-up world. After it sunk in, I just sat, staring into the darkness, needing water, needing another cigarette, but not ready to move yet. After all, there was no one watching now.

When I went upstairs and typed 'transgender,' into a search engine, it asked, 'Did you mean transcended?' That's how it felt, what Tyler did – elusive, controlled, on her own terms, and without me.

It hadn't been a pleasant letter – its opening, 'I don't know if you knew…' was as soft as it got. There were pages of defences and justifications, wrapped in Tyler's usual crackling off-handedness. Admittedly, I was recently divorced, I'd said goodbye to my only child and so I was bordering on insane, but never has 'I don't know,' sounded so much like, 'I don't care.' I'd lost her again and I hadn't even known I could.

Him. I have to get used to saying that. I'd lost him.

*

On the fourth day of Jess's higher education, when I didn't think I could handle waiting another week to see her, let alone two months, I finally got a phone call from Tyler Corrigan. I expected very little, and certainly not this benediction, husky with twenty years of unfiltered tobacco. His voice spilled across my desk like a flood of unasked-for sun.

Tyler was blunt as ever, but friendly. As we talked, I thought of all those letters I'd thrust aside, even the latest one, and realised that he hadn't meant any of them to hurt me; hearing that voice wasn't just a blessing, but a pardon – and having always been deep and smoke-cured, at least it sounded familiar.

'I know it's short notice and all, but I'm in town for a couple days and the firm's got a box at the Proms . . . meetings and such during the day, now we're drinking and partying with middle-class Brits. I think the excitement's actually gonna kill me. What are you doing tonight?' I heard his lighter click. 'You want to save my life?'

In a moment of madness, perhaps brought on by splurging on a bottle of champagne at a two hundred per cent mark-up outside Knightsbridge Tube, I bought a single calla lily from a stall, as pale and curved as my twenty-year-old flesh. I thought of pinning it to my lapel, but instead I twisted it into my hair. Only Tyler would notice my little floral tribute. No one else looked at women like me.

Walking up to the Albert Hall, its stone steps basking in the evening sun, I felt myself grow lighter. This was the first thing I'd done, in months of purgatory, that was purely for pleasure. No legal paperwork, no recriminations- just the white flower in my hair, the cold bottleneck sweating in my hand, and the dandyish figure at the top of the stairs, so sharply outlined that it made me feel dishevelled. A new man.

Tyler was charming, attentive – a real Southern gentleman. The champagne hit my bloodstream right away, crystals shattering into vapour on my tongue. I relaxed; I was here, I was broken from the divorce, it was temporary, and that was fine.

As we settled in the box with Tyler's junior staff around us, he whispered in my ear, 'Don't worry. I feel great now.'

'I wish I'd been there,' I said, not knowing what I meant- in America, at the surgery, in his life at all?

He was already consulting the programme. 'Beethoven Night. We're in for a treat, or so they say. If it gets bad, can you wake me up?'

'Do you still play?'

He nodded. 'Yeah, but . . . mainly just for me.'

The music hit our faces like a subway wind. I remembered Tyler at the piano on a summer evening, muttering through a jet of fragrant smoke, 'Y'know, all the best music begins in the middle.' It was like birth, a thunderous thrusting right into the heart of it all.

Within half an hour of Beethoven, I was all of my selves at once; twelve, falling off my bike and skinning both knees; twenty-one, striding through bar-rooms in a backless gown; twenty-three, wringing my young husband's hand like laundry as the baby came; forty and sobbing on the bathroom floor.

The bubbles' chemical sweetness mingled with salt. Tyler pressed a white handkerchief into my hand though his eyes were welling too, pearly skin mottling with colour.

'Hormones,' he muttered, startling a laugh out of me.

We hurtled into and beyond the music, eyes shut, hands clasped, barely breathing. The orchestra in their white shirts were as dazzling as a fleet of ships in front of us, the music a greedy headlong rush into the light, like my daughter's first cry. No time to learn, rehearse, or stop and breathe. We were already late, born into this motion with no choice but to ride it out. It was as though we had always suspected this, and here it was at last, the proof we'd been waiting for.

With the house empty, and between Tyler's business trips, we slowly let something happen. Now we go to the clubs, applaud some of the old jazzers and drink with their fans – middle-aged, middle-class record collectors pausing as Tyler slides viper-smooth through the chairs, 'All right, mate?' We haven't run into anyone we know yet.

Tyler has to live with his hands, his height; short, for a guy. I chose my own, much smaller permanent mark. My tattoo, the first bars of those 'Transcendental Etudes' of his, a ribbon of music on my back where his fingers pool. A fence of notes with little feminine flourishes, put there by a girl my daughter's age with tribal plugs in her ears.

There's no proof that night at the Godin Hall ever happened- no playbills, no reviews, but we do have this. The music, stripped back to flesh and bone. In the dark, Tyler feels his way over the notes, humming, as though drawing the music out of my skin.

Towards Christmas, I mark the dates on the calendar; the end of Jess's first term, and his next visit. I know Jess is tired of grown-ups telling her how quickly time passes, the hunger we get in our faces when we buttonhole her, begging her not to waste a moment. I can refrain from reminding her about that. I am her mother, after all. I can count the days for all of us.

THE FUCK IT LIST

THE FUCK IT LIST

ANGELA CLERKIN

She can hear the sound of the sea and the velvet voice of a beautiful woman whispering in her ear.

Today you are exactly halfway through. Are you the person you are supposed to be? Have all your childhood dreams come true, Siobhan? Or are you surplus to requirements? Will it all be downhill from now on? Have you already missed the boat? 18th July 2057, Siobhan O'Malley RIP'.

Siobhan sits bolt upright gasping for breath. She is sweating. The bedroom is dark, but at least it is her bedroom and it was just a dream. No need to panic, she tells her quickened heartbeat. She wonders for a brief moment if Monique had been playing a trick on her, but her girlfriend is sleeping soundly next to her, not stirring. Besides, that isn't Monique's style, trying to scare her with cruel insights and predictions. The immigration solicitor is a practical, no-nonsense person – they both are.

18th July 2057. How specific, she ponders, how bizarre. Siobhan tries to work out how old that would make on her death day, but it is too early for her sleepy brain. She used to be good at mental arithmetic but with the advent of calculators her faculties aren't quite so sharp. Perhaps it is all downhill from now on, she thinks.

The digital clock flashes 4.30am in red when Siobhan presses the button, announcing that today has already arrived. The worries of work flood into her mind, drowning out the velvet voice. Redundancies are due to be announced at the office soon, and Angus, her boss at the advertising company, has confided the names of those to face the chop. Not as he said because he trusts and values Siobhan more than his wife, but, she suspects, because he wanted her to carry some of the guilt. Every day Siobhan faces questions from colleagues asking about their futures, Joanne has only just bought a flat and Derrick's wife is expecting their third baby. And meanwhile her own oft promised raise hasn't materialised, ('count yourself lucky you still have a job'), she is the oldest person in the office by at least ten years, (time to dye the hair again) and her job with prospects has become just a job.

There is no possibility of sleep now, Siobhan admits, at least not without a comforting hot chocolate to sooth her. She steps out onto the cold wooden floor, grabs her fluffy pink dressing gown from the back of the door and quietly goes down stairs.

Numerous files marked Helima Anwar lie on top of last night's *Evening Standard*, Siobhan transfers them to Monique's desk in the adjoining room. The solicitors all-consuming work irritatingly spreading all over their house, all over their relationship. Siobhan finds herself looking at her girlfriend's advice notes on the asylum seeker's case and is reminded of why she first became attracted to her thirteen years ago. Monique's unrelenting energy and determination to help those who need protection and have their voices heard. And of course those delicious chocolate button eyes and tiny afro didn't go unnoticed.

At the table Siobhan sips her lukewarm cocoa and flicks through yesterday's so-called news and what will appropriately become today's bin liner. The article 'Childhood dreams' catches her eye and she stiffens as she reads the first sentence: In a survey by Learn Direct 97% of people in their 40s said their childhood dreams haven't come true. The velvet voice rings in her ears, *'Have all your childhood dreams come true, Siobhan?'*

When I was nine I dreamt of being a saint. I read all about the lives of the saints and decided to choose one to be my inspiration. In the running was Wilgerfortis who grew a beard, Agnes who cut off her breasts, Theresa who as far as I understood didn't do anything special except eat cheese, and Apollonia who lost all her teeth. I decided on Theresa who ate the cheese. Every day I would cut a very thin slice of my mother's blue vein, poisonous-looking cheese, and make myself eat it, running to the bathroom immediately afterwards to brush my teeth and obliterate the revolting taste. I waited patiently, month after month, masticating away, hoping Jesus was looking and would recognise I had the makings of a saint. When I was nine I knew I was special even if nobody else did.

Siobhan was the eldest of six children to James and Kathleen O'Malley in Malahide, a small seaside town not far from Dublin. She had ventured to London in her early twenties to study English literature at university and she adored the big metropolis from the moment she arrived. No-one watched her every move, no-one knew every member of her family, no-one was keen to report back any transgression. And the young woman planned many a transgression, she had been obsessing about girls ever since she first fell in love with blonde Clare with the jam-jar glasses at school. The freedom of London was liberating but frightening to Siobhan at times. Too many possibilities, too many things that could go wrong, and who would be there to catch her? Fear was something in her genes and it appeared that no amount of travelling miles or crossing seawater was ever going to change that. But her love of London just about out-weighed the fear of the unfamiliar, the uncontrollable, and so she stayed.

In the past decade she returned home for three funerals. She found her mother and two brother's deaths totally heartbreaking. However her formerly belligerent father had softened, and Siobhan's relationship with him began to flourish with their shared love of James Joyce and WB Yeats. They would speak on the phone almost every week and she received medical updates (and family gossip) from her surviving siblings via Facebook.

Rushing to board the Liverpool train, clasping three heavy lever arch files, and an almond croissant, Monique's thoughts are with the woman whom she hopes to save, or at least delay, from deportation. Already forgotten is the note Siobhan left on the table saying she had woken early but would see her the following night on Monique's return from Merseyside. The solicitor had also emptied her mind of the earlier irritation that her girlfriend had not only moved her carefully ordered legal papers, but the greedy cow had also finished all the cereal. She knew that she was being unfair but that was how she felt when she found the cupboard bare. Anyway in her book 'unfair' is more about how the system fucks people over when they have already been through unimaginable trauma, not who blames who for forgetting to put porridge on the shopping list. Helima Anwar will be relying on her expertise today and Monique, all guns blazing, is on the 8.35am chariot northward bound.

On the other hand Angus was incensed by his employee's text claiming illness. He had to concede the reliable Ms O'Malley had barely had a day off sick since she joined the company fourteen years ago. However this morning was inconvenient, he had a meeting scheduled with HR and Joanne Peterson. He wanted his office manager to soak up the emotional mess that would inevitably ensue. Some people need to grow thicker skins, and other people need to look after their health better, he thought as he ran his hand through his thinning red hair and poured himself a wee tot of Jameson's. He allowed himself one whisky with his breakfast since his wife had left him three months ago and he was more or less keeping to it. 'Marsha in accounts is quite motherly, she can mop up the tears today,' he decided when he saw the bottom of his glass.

Meanwhile, Siobhan was getting off the fast train to Brighton and wondering what the hell she was doing there. Then the glistening sea waved at her from the bottom of the hill and she began to walk down towards it. On the journey from London, as she had watched trees and matchbox houses whizzing past through smudged windows, she thought about all her reasons to feel guilty. It was quite a list. She reached for her phone to check on her father as promised but instead she turned it off and put it back in her bag.

The reflection in the train window shows her long dark hair is beginning to grey at the temples. Lines have started to engrave her white porcelain skin, revealing the wear and tear of life. Siobhan loves wrinkly faces, the lines telling their wearer's history, but she doesn't like her own being quite so obvious. She wishes she had left her melancholy back in London.

Walking along the seafront Siobhan loves the fact that it is raining and the beach is deserted. Just her footprints in the sand and her sadness blowing in the wind. She ambles along the narrow lanes and stops to stare at the Pavillion. The beautiful, absurd building makes her smile. She decides that the architect must have just said 'fuck it, I'll do what I want.' Audacious and extravagant, that takes confidence, she thinks.

After fighting off seagulls trying to swoop in on her fish and chips as she sat eating on the pebbled beach, Siobhan strolls onto the pier. She resists offers of candy floss and having her name written in Chinese on a scroll. But as she walks past an old-fashioned gypsy caravan advertising 'Tarot reading and Clairvoyance' she slows down and retraces her steps.

Inside the red scarves and gold lanterns hanging from the rounded ceiling make Siobhan smile. The little woman sitting behind the small table looks like a fabulous character from a 70s spy movie, wearing an expensive dark purple velvet suit, a leopard skin print silk shirt and silver sling backs. Her short, white hair frames her very lined face as if it is a work of art. The elderly woman's eyes sparkle with devilment, enormous silver hooped earrings hang from her lobes and there is a smile or perhaps a smirk dancing around the corner of her red lipsticked mouth.

'Darlink, sadly ve must discuss ze business first. You pay cash or card?' I wonder if the accent is for real but say nothing. I pass her my credit card as I like to keep a record of how I spend my money. She inserts it into her handheld machine and I wryly comment, 'It's the modern age,' but she doesn't reply. I was finding this whole situation bizarre, I'm not usually one to give into whims like this. She asks me to put in my pin number and it crosses my mind this is some sort of a con and I should have paid cash. Too late now, I will have to keep an eye on my bank account over the next few days. She returns my card to me and places two packs of tarot cards and a handful of stones and crystals onto the gold table cloth.

'Hold zee's cards and shuffle zem.'

She instructs me in what sounds like a passable impression of Zsa Zsa Gabor. I pick up the tarot cards and they feel surprising large in my hands.

'Sink about your life over ze past year. Now bring into your conscious mind your dreams for ze next twelve months. Continue to shuffle ze cards. Now tell me ze first thing that enters your mind'

'I feel as if I have missed the boat,' I admit quietly. She gently takes the cards from my hands and puts them down without laying them out.

'What boat was that you missed?' she asks as she reaches out and tucks my hair behind my ears. I am slightly taken aback by the familiarity of her gesture but I continue my flow of thought regardless.

'The career boat. The successful woman boat. The boat named after me that means I am somebody, that somebody cared enough to name a boat after me. The boat of motherhood. Not that I'm sure I actually wanted to get on that one. The boat of opportunities, and pastures new. The boat that everyone else seems to be on except me.'

'Zome people are on the Titantic – do you wish to be on zat boat?'

I see a hint of a smirk on her lips as she lights up a pink Sobranie cigarette. I want to grab it off her and stub it out. Tell her to quit with the smart come-backs, I am doing my best here. But I don't say or do anything. I have just paid £20 and I don't want to waste it.

'You are angry, frustrated,' (she's got that right, smoke in my eyes. Isn't smoking at a place of work illegal?) 'But most of all you are stuck.'

Through gritted teeth I announce I feel I am here under false pretences. There doesn't seem to be much clairvoyance going on, she hasn't even looked at the cards. I don't say that I am feeling foolish for confiding my innermost fears to a complete stranger in a crappy caravan. The fortune teller laughs, she is enjoying herself. She takes a couple more drags on her cocktail cigarette and looks me in the eyes. Her eyes are a beautiful hazel colour, like a cat. How old is this woman? The lines suggest perhaps mid-late 60s, a full and adventurous life led, that's for sure. Then she leans forward, and takes my hand in hers.

'You feel as if you are surplus to requirements. Zat it is all downhill from now on. And because I haven't told you that you will come into a fortune and meet a tall, handsome stranger you worry you are being ripped off. So what if you are? You can afford twenty pounds, Siobhan. Relax and enjoy zee ride.'

A bottle of Jack Daniels and a couple of shot glasses that are inscribed 'Fiesta' and have pictures of ladies wearing lime green bikinis and extravagant headdresses appear from under the table. How could I resist? We knock two back in quick succession and then she produces a box of dark chocolates from the oriental cabinet behind her. I obligingly open my mouth as she holds one to my lips. She laughs, 'Zis is better! Now Gloria's turn. Feed me!'

With a mouthful of chocolate Gloria got up and tottered over in her silver sling-backs to hang the closed sign outside the caravan door. 'It's down tools for the day. Time to live a little,' she said in her real cockney accent. Siobhan smiled. Gloria's laugh caught in her throat and released a painful sounding smoker's cough. 'When I get blue,' she continued, 'first thing I do is make sure I tell another human being, which you've just done, and then I get out my 'fuck it' list.' She turned to the oriental cabinet and this time produced a crumpled piece of paper from a drawer. 'Pick a number,' she demanded, 'Three', Siobhan promptly replied. The old lady grinned and said, 'Perfect! Coat back on, we're off out.' This turn of events was quite unexpected but the office manager decided to go with the flow, today was after all a stolen day from work.

I was head-back, full laughing, holding tightly onto the wheel of the speed boat. I looked ridiculous wearing the black eye patch Gloria had just given me, and she was quoting Yeats at me in broad cockney, 'Come away, O human child: To the waters and the wild with a fairy, hand in hand'.

A young Spanish student on the pier stood looking over the white iron railings as two ladies sped by on a boat below screaming and laughing. She noticed that one of them was wearing an eye patch and the other a dark purple suit and silver shoes. Rosita felt relieved that there seemed to be crazy lesbians-a-plenty in this little English town, she should fit in well.

Gloria grabs the steering wheel and pulls it down to the right. Suddenly the boat is tilting as it curves round, causing the sea to rear up playfully. The wave kindly crashes down the other side so we escape a soaking. In retaliation I decide to pull the wheel down sharply to the left, but I nearly capsize us. Gloria falls into me and as I catch her arm I realise how thin and frail she really is. She smiles but looks a little shocked so I make sure the fairy-woman holds onto the wheel tightly with both of her boney hands. I stand closely behind her, my warm arms wrapped around her, my strong hands steadying the wheel.

We don't speak for ages, I don't want to break the spell. The fierce wind is blowing away the cobwebs in my brain. Emptying out the rubbish from tucked away corners, where useless and dark messages have taken root. My body feels sure and my heart content. I belong here on the sea.

*

'I am going to call you Grace from now on. The eye patch suits you.' Gloria informed Siobhan as they sat drinking cappuccinos in a café on St James's Street. The silver-haired woman began to regale tales of an Irish female pirate from the 16th century. Stories of wildness, bravery and recklessness took them right through two coffees and a shared piece of walnut cake. 'Grace O'Malley made sure she never missed a boat,' concluded Gloria. 'Well she did own a whole fleet of them,' added Siobhan. The elderly woman narrowed her eyes and grinned, recognizing her protégé had been humouring her. The Irish woman told her cockney companion about her home-town Malahide and how much she missed living by the sea. Much of her early years were mis-spent with her sisters and brothers playing pirates on the old abandoned fishing boats.

The café was closing for the day. Gloria took a mobile phone from her silver clutch bag and announced it was time for her new friend to meet her grandson.

As they walked slowly uphill enroute to Franco's shop the old woman was telling Siobhan that she should have chosen Wilgerfortis as her role model rather then St Theresa. 'She is truer to your nature, darling. You felt different. The bearded lady would have brought you pride.' Siobhan was enjoying the fact that this hilarious cockney might be a total washout as a clairvoyant but she was fantastic company, and well worth the twenty quid.

It wasn't until the needle was actually piercing the flesh in her upper arm that Siobhan had second thoughts about the wisdom of what she was doing. Franco, Gloria's grandson, was a tattooist. When he read the doubt on Siobhan O'Malley's face he sang 'Relax' by Frankie Goes To

Hollywood at the top of his considerable lungs to take her mind off the pain and her foolishness. The proud grandmother reminded Siobhan that it's essential to make a few mistakes in life otherwise lessons will never be learnt. 'And your bleeding drawing, love, that Franco's copying, is a big fat mistake!' Siobhan laughed and replied 'Fuck it. I love it!' Siobhan was happy that Wilgerfortis, the patron saint of bearded ladies, was going to be with her from here on in.

The vintage Mary Quant dress that Gloria had chosen for me so that we could achieve number six on the list was fantastic. 'I am not wearing that! No way can I get away with showing off my legs, at my age!' I protested as I was climbing into the dress at the back of the tattooists. Gloria had nipped home to select my outfit while Franco explained that his Nan had been a fashion stylist in the 60s and 70s and had an amazing clothing collection, which he and his friends regularly raided. I took some convincing to go clubbing as number six on the 'fuck it' list required. But my companions were adamant. The tattooist insisted Wilgerfortis needed to see Brighton's night-life before venturing to London on my arm. How could I argue with that?

'Just throw some shapes' and 'Embrace your eccentricities' were the words of encouragement shouted at Siobhan on the way into the noisy, dark, mixed gay/straight club. The little blue pill that the middle-aged Irish woman halved with 'Nan' meant that Siobhan danced for three hours and forgot there was any other time except now.

Gloria had wisely sat on the roof garden of the club with her Sobranies and an entourage of gay men for most of the night. She was still keen to continue the adventure when Siobhan eventually found her at 2am. They walked through the narrow lanes with Gloria holding onto Siobhan's non-tattooed arm, and Siobhan holding onto her shoes. Her feet were killing her and walking barefoot on the cobbles was clearly a challenge that triggered much teasing from the tough as old boots pensioner. 'How comes you're still managing to wear heels this time of night?!' 'I sleep with them on, darling, they're glued to my feet.'

Gloria pointed out a circular sign like a large love-heart sweet in the window of the furniture and design shop which said, *Never forget how to kiss.* 'I want that for my kitchen, it will remind me that the table is not just for serving food on!' Gloria laughed and laughed with delight at this thought. Siobhan said nothing; a little sadness had crept into her heart. Siobhan hadn't even kissed her longtime girlfriend goodbye before she left. Some of their passion had been buried in practicalities and habit.

We are walking along the pier as Gloria takes out a quarter bottle of rum from her silver clutch bag. Swigging the warming alcohol, we perch on the steps of her caravan. She tells me about missing her daughter, and the loneliness that sometimes chokes her. At first I think she means Janice is dead, but as she continues I realise Franco's mother has disappeared off the radar due to heroin. Gloria recounts episodes of trying to cope, mend, and survive the ugliness of addiction. She talks about her daughter's fantastic but self destructive spirit and the pain of watching someone take the 'fuck it' mentality to such an extreme she isn't just throwing the baby out with the bath water, she is throttling it until there is no breath left.

And as Gloria talks I watch her make a small boat out of a paper napkin from the club. She takes a lipstick out of her silver clutch bag, inscribes the letter 'J' on the boat, and slips it inside the now empty quarter bottle of rum. Flinging the bottle off the end of the pier into the sea she says, 'You never know, Janice might find the bottle one day and know that somebody cared enough about her to name a boat after her. Isn't that what you said you wanted earlier?' I put my arm around the vulnerable old lady's shoulder and tease, 'Or she might just think her mother's a sentimental old lush!' Her deep laugh makes her whole body shudder. Gloria reaches into her silver clutch bag for her cigarettes and lights up two Sobranies. The two of us puff away as we promenade beside the moonlit sea, arm in arm.

Apparently Franco has phoned ahead, on his grandmother's instructions, and booked me a room with a sea view – no expense spared – I can afford it, she says. Gloria insists on walking me all the way into the reception area. As we say goodbye I hug her so tight, I don't want to let go. Then she kisses me on the mouth, gently. 'Never forget how to kiss, Siobhan' she says, and she kisses me again. I watch glorious Gloria disappear out of my sight through the revolving door. I retire upstairs to my queen-sized bed in the Queen's hotel and sleep soundly in the shape of a starfish in the middle of the bed.

On the train back to London the following morning Siobhan sat at a table with a take-away tea and a pen and paper. Before she turned her mobile back on to receive the five messages from Monique varying from 'Can you buy some more porridge?' to 'Sweetheart, I can't wait to see you!' Siobhan began to write.

Siobhan's Fuck It List :

1. Go disco dancing and not care that I am too old. (Or that I call it disco dancing)

2. I nominate tomorrow for swear-a-lot day.

3. Take risks – I'm not going to die until 2057 – Do a parachute jump, drive a racing car, learn to surf, go skateboarding etc.

4. Visit Ratha, the nine year old girl I sponsor in Cambodia and see her life, what it is really like for her.

5. Never forget how to kiss – take Monique to McDonald's and snog til we are thrown out or someone says 'get a room'. And then get a room.

6. Wear an eye patch or a false beard to work.

7. Buy a dress designed by Vivienne Westwood and wear it.

8. Confront my uncle and not worry about upsetting other people.

9. Admit the dream: I am going to write the great Irish novel of the 21st century – take three months off work and live in a cottage near the Ring of Kerry and write. Or not write and just enjoy.

10. One day a month is 'fuck it' day. Phone off, no emails and do something irresponsible.

A PARTRIDGE IN A PEAR TREE

A PARTRIDGE IN A PEAR TREE

STELLA DUFFY

When the King of Spain's daughter came to visit me she wore a gown of ivory brocade cut into with diamond lace. On her feet were calfskin shoes and she carried a fan carved from a single elephant tusk. The King of Spain's daughter travelled from Seville to Cordoba by foot, then by carriage to Madrid. She waited two hours at the airport there, bought a Steven King novel and caught an adjoining flight to Barcelona. Unfortunately she left the book – just three chapters in and already dog-eared – in the seat-back pocket on the plane. After a brief diversionary weekend in Sitges, lunch in Tarragona, supper in Girona, she travelled the coast road up to Perpignan. I did not know she was coming, but on the day she left, a week after the feast of the Assumption, I knew something was on its way. I felt it in the water, washed my hands in a porcelain bowl and the cool liquid was heavy with waiting.

I will come to you in the evening, orange blossom in my hair. I will take your hand and hold it to my breast, you will count the beats of my heart. We will never go astray. Daylight may be marred by fog or rain, the moon waxes and wanes, the earth spins on an elliptical axis so that even the rising sun appears to arrive from an altered direction, adjusting the angle of shine from summer to winter. But the Pole Star and the Southern Cross have marked us out. I'm coming. I'll need a cup of tea when I get there. And a good book.

I don't know how she found me. I know why she found me. The tree drew her, of course. Pear tree, not nut tree, no matter what they called it. I should know, I planted the seed. It drew them all, my little tree. Cousins and kings, councillors, counts, and the others too. Those that would steal it, take the harvest, smelt it down, make their own precious things. There are always people waiting to steal what they can, especially from something as generous as my little tree – those welcoming wide open branches. But these were my precious things, they would not be taken. Having planted the seed in the first place – one part organic compost to two parts peat and sand mix - I too was surprised when the tree began. I remember my fifth form biology, I eat bean sprouts, I know what to watch for.

I know what to watch for. The lie of the land, sleight of hand, wedding band. Your ring finger is empty. I will fill it for you.

I watched the seed unfurl and grow. And keep growing. First the kitchen windowsill, then a gentle tempering to the outdoors, terracotta pot bubble-wrapped tight for chilly evenings, by spring the root and branches were strong enough for the ground. London clay, thick and cloying, seemed worth a try. The blossom arrived first. It was not as I had expected, almost too delicate. We had a warm spring this year, lucky spring, a late and easy Easter, four full moons packed into the first three months. I know about trees, fruit and nut. Have read up on them, our local library sees a lot of allotmenteers, books pock-marked by dirty fingers. Usually there must be two trees, male and female, for the promiscuous dancing bees. I had just the one. It wasn't meant to fruit so soon. But it did. How it did. Nutmeg and pear. Pear tree with a little added spice.

I agree with you. After all, if the tree blooms a pear, then surely the branch on which it sits is a pear tree? And pear wood is mine, always has been. Sacred to Athena, Hera, Vishnu-Narayana. (I looked it up online.) I am coming for it. For the gardener too and your rough dirt-working hands. I don't mind a hard journey. I do not believe it is better to travel than to arrive, at least not in second class accommodation. But the approach is valuable, a time of preparation, consideration. I gather myself, the advent of arrival.

Unfortunately one of my neighbours, nosy woman, always chatting over the fence, became interested in the tree's progress. It is the curse of our London terraces – you think I live here because I actually enjoy a recreation of the fifties myth, street-party stories? I certainly do not. Sadly I do not have the wealth to garner anonymity and my interfering neighbour saw the shining leaves. I had tried to shield the heavy flowers from her spying eyes, the prying spies I knew she would tell, a full mouth of secrets dripping from the corner of her curling lips. I built a shed around the tree, open to summer light, closed against winter dark. Glass roofed, glass bricked, creosote-edged beams erected merely for the scent, my shed was a place of translucent light and slow growing ease. I am no DIY expert, B&Q is close to the seventh ring of hell for me, IKEA a Swedish prison. But I tried hard, worked harder and, in the end, I was pretty damn pleased with the result. There are people who enjoy the process of creation. Not me, my moment of satisfaction comes from having it all done and dusted. Ready. Waiting.

I dressed well for the journey, packed better for my arrival. We had some troubles on the way, problems both with transport and accommodation. You have to pre-book Travel Inns far in advance these days and I prefer not to give out my credit card details on the telephone if at all possible, I do not easily believe in strangers. Well, but not easily. Still, we managed. I wore the silk brocade, dark green. It creases least of all my gowns. The diamond cuts can be perilous though, the edges are carbon-dated and sharp. As long as I take care to move with precision my skin generally stays whole. And the calf-skin slippers are very soft, easy to walk in. I have read the new suggestion that even short journeys can cause deep-vein thrombosis, it is best to take precautions. I dance in my slippers whenever possible. Airline stewards usually appreciate the gesture.

Summer took its time and the blossom turned to fruit, growing full and fatter by the day, weighing down the fine branches. There was so much interest I gave in eventually, took the neighbour's interference as an opportunity instead. I offered tickets at my front door, a glimpse of the silver and gold for a tenner. For many of them that was enough. I could still feel her in my waters, it was growing heavier by the day. I worried for the meter, thick sticky ticking through the massy wet. The bill from our beloved Thames Water would no doubt be excessive, and I'd stopped going to work to guard the tree. The universe was perilously close to giving up providing. My quarterly council tax was due as well, gate sales were good, but possibly not quite enough for Lambeth's exorbitance. But still I sat, in the cut-glass shed. I knew something was coming, someone. I trusted her to make it all better. And I trusted my tree. It would not give its treasures up to just anyone, nor offer the fruit to any hand.

I wear a ring on my left hand. Daughter of Athena, the owl that watches from my ring finger itches in a straight line to my heart. Summer grows hotter and the central plains are arid. We travel on, further north. I trust you are worth my journey. (All journeys travel on trust.)

Late summer turned to autumn slipped into the harvest festival, full moon and she on her way.

I can smell you. Your spice scent dragged me up through France, the TGV faster still for my nose's demands. Silver nutmeg in a hot toddy, silver nutmeg mixed into smooth mashed potato, silver nutmeg grated on rice pudding. You will remove the ugly milk skin before I see it, I know you will. The comfort dishes of my desire have dragged me drugged with aroma through the Channel Tunnel. Just twenty minutes and a cheering group of school children to cross under water into the sceptred isle, I dance the aisle and smile on England. Aquitaine's Eleanor would have loved this. Though perhaps she was more of a cinnamon girl.

There is a pear too you know. Juicy pear, ripe pear. An always-ripe pear. Never too hard, never too soft, just right little Goldilocks, this pear is always just right. It will not rot nor drop from the tree. Well, you wouldn't expect any less from a golden one, would you? Not gilded you understand, but actually, truly, properly gold. So why all the fuss about the silver nutmeg? There is also a glistening gleaming golden pear. That's a big deal too isn't it? I tell you Marco Polo, the spice route has a lot to answer for.

Slowing down now for the Kent countryside, hops picked, apples stored in cool barns. And then houses become clustered, back gardens open their faces to morning-tired commuters, the train steadies me forward to Waterloo winter and tube tickets and escalator and lift and change to overground train and then street and 45 bus and you. Your house. Your garden shed of glass. So this is it. I am come. I ring the bell.

The doorbell is ringing. I can hear it. My little tree can hear it too, the sap rises. Nutmeg and pear sing softly to themselves, ringing through their metal. She has arrived, our very own personal pronoun of what happens next. I was eager before, nervous but eager, now I am just scared. What if I don't like her? What if she doesn't like me? What if I don't matter and all the fuss is, yet again, only for the tree? The doorbell is ringing. I rise from my ripped yellow stool – its plastic coating once matched a fine fifties formica table – and open the shed door. It has been raining. I've been in here since last light last night and now there are spider webs in my way. Picked out in individual wet droplets, crossing my path. The strung webs are pretty, in a modernist Christmas decoration, silver-and-plain-crystal-nothing-too-gaudy, kind of way. They are also a sticky nuisance as I walk back into the house, through the kitchen, down the hall to the front door, leaving a dozen homeless spiders behind me as I go. I'll say this for the King of Spain's daughter, she certainly knows how to ring a bell.

The door opens away from me and you are just as I expected. Tall and lean and the tanned skin of your face is fine-etched from the many hours of gardening and building work during the long summer. You are beautiful, but then I would not have expected less. The seed would not have pushed through the dirt unless it wanted to take a good look at you. I stand on your doorstep, looking over your shoulder into the hall. Your house is a little more suburban than I would have thought. That dado rail will have to go. And I'm not sure about the coir matting covering the stripped and sanded floorboards. I know they are appropriate for the area, your age and your social group, but isn't it rough on bare feet first thing in the morning? We shall see.

She was short. I knew she was short because I had to lower my eye level when I opened the door. For some reason I had expected a taller woman. Dark, with long hair and longer limbs. The flamenco dancer classic I guess. Not that she wasn't beautiful. And the orange blossom was a good touch. She did have the long dark hair, dark skin, big round brown eyes – a young Susan Dey, after the braces and the faked piano playing, and many years before LA Law turned her blonde. I was a bit rubbish there, at the door, just staring. It's not every day I greet royalty on my doorstep. The Queen doesn't come south of the river all that often, can't get the cabs I expect. I wasn't sure how to address her. Your highness. Your holiness. Darling.

You stand aside and I enter. I am used to a little more ceremony in welcome, but you will learn in time. I will teach you. I am a good teacher, have schooled both willing and unwilling pupils. Between us there is a shy glance, sly glance, and I note your dilating pupils. Mine too I expect. We have both felt the strong desire stretching from here to my home, reaching halfway across this continent. As I journeyed closer our joint passion compacted, a black hole into which all wanting poured. My suitcases are piled beside your wheelie bin, you pay the porters from my Lulu Guinness purse, take the bags in your hands and then begin a stumble of uncertainty. Upstairs or downstairs, where is my lady's chamber? You are reticent and do not know which room to show me first. I lead the way, unerring sense of direction, up the stairs, first right and into the bathroom. No bidet, how English. I wash my travel-dirtied hands. Your water is heavy, isn't it? Is that what they mean by the limescale problem here? We will install filters. Next week. For now I take your builder's hands, gardener's hands, hold them in mine which are clean and a little wet still. There is a hardened blister just north of your lifeline. I will smooth that, soothe that, my tongue reaches for the scrape of rough skin. You are coy, slow, I hear an intake of breath and smile. There is time. How about a cup of tea?

She unpacked, I put the kettle on. I was just starting to worry that perhaps she'd want some girlie herbal tea and all I had were builders' bags, when she walked into the kitchen carrying a small wooden chest. She had changed, jeans and a t-shirt. But she still wore the calf-skin slippers. Fair enough, that diamond lace looked dangerous. Lovely, but dangerous. She sat the chest on the kitchen table and showed it to me. It was well made, old. There were nine drawers, each one lined in silver with a different faintly scented selection of fine leaves. She took the pot from me – our fingers crossed again – and began to mix her brew. Half a teaspoon of this, a quarter of that, one full of another. Each one dropped into the pot, falling with a gentle shush. Then the boiling water and then the wait. Five minutes she said. Long enough to take a good long look. I thought she meant the tree, opened the back door, pointed the way past the ripped and hanging webs. She did not follow. It was not yet time. She meant me, I was to be looked at. Inspected is not too fine a definition for the looking that began again with my hands, lingered on my forearms, dwelt on my shoulders and back and neck and then came to my face.

I want to see you. See what they do not see when they sweep past you and out to the little tree. I want to see the one who planted the seed.

She touched my eyelids and the delicate veined skin yearned to open for her. She ran the back of a smooth-buffed thumbnail across my eyelashes and each one blinked for her, severally and individually. She traced the print of her index finger along my eyebrows and down to the tired shadows of my long waiting - I knew for the first time the perfect circularity of my eye sockets. She lingered with the quiet wrinkles at the time–folded corners, laughter lines, worry lines, crying lines. I could have told her the content of each one. She did not ask. And then, finally, she licked the ball of her left little finger and brought her own liquid to my dry tear duct. It was a surprise and a relief. The tea was ready. We had a cup each. And chocolate bourbons. They were new to her. She ate five and a half.

When I kiss you the taste on your tongue is of these English biscuits. They are nice, plain. Later I will feed you on my food. When I lick your hand the flavour is of your garden, London clay and spider's webs, clean and dirty at the same time. When you hold me I am nearly naked. For a woman used to boned corsets, wide dresses, heavy gowns, this t-shirt is flimsy and easily removed. (Remove it easily.) When we lie together on your kitchen floor I wonder in passing about the cleanliness, how recently this room was swept do you have a cleaner will you clean for me wash for me touch for me love for me. I wonder in passing and then you are passing over my body around my skin under my heart and I into you and you back to me and this is why I have come, why I am here, where I will come back to. You are easy, quiet, slow, ready. The wait was worth it, I hear the song of bending boughs from the shed at the bottom of your garden.

I'd never had sex with royalty before either. Fortunately the protocols weren't all that different. She was smooth and soft except just at the waistband where the diamond lace had cut into her, leaving a lattice of small scratches, light scabs for gently easing free. When we were done with the kissing and the turning and the laying and the wanting we went upstairs together to wash. I ran her a bath and she lay back into the water. It was heavy and held her close. I would have climbed in with her, but she said that would not be right. Not on a first date. I showered when she was finished, cleaned the tub and wiped it down. I pulled her long black hairs from the plug hole, dried, combed and plaited them. Put away the thin rope of hair in a heart-shaped music box left behind by my last lover.

You are storing me, shoring me up, just in case. There is no need. I'm staying now.

She said she was hungry again, that travelling always gave her an appetite and the airline food appeared to have become even worse since the imposition of further security checks.

I don't mind the security, really I don't, I appreciate both the necessity and the effort involved, but I am very disturbed by that whole plastic cutlery thing.

She said she needed flesh, meat, wanted to suck small bones. I offered a frozen chicken from the freezer, fish fingers maybe, but she had come prepared. Pulled enamel pots and aluminium pans from the Luis Vuitton, condiments and utensils from her handbag, and an A-Z from her pocket. The shops were all open for her, workmen left their waiting on this ordinary extraordinary day. Her presence keeps us all willing working. It's a good trick. No doubt explains her hometown's impressively balanced budget. We went to Stockwell Road where she haggled with an elderly Portuguese man, two small boys watching in admiration. Walked Streatham High Street from Brixton Hill to the ice rink. Finally took a half-empty train to Borough Market and came home with our afternoon arms full of essential provisions. The birds are small and firm and clean. A small white feather floats down as I open the gate.

(Came home? I like that.) I will make you Toledo partridge with dark chocolate sauce.

I eat the chocolate, she grates it into my hand, hard and bitter, it wakens the edges of my tongue. She needs one glass of dry white wine for the dish. We keep back a glass each for ourselves and pour the rest at the base of the tree. Moisture enough for a London winter.

According to the old man in the high street shop, this bird laid fifteen eggs in one day. She was one of his finest, will do well for Catalan-style partridge, ten garlic gloves fat and pink, two dozen onions, not one of them larger than the O of your open-mouthed love.

She peels each onion carefully, stripping back the finest layer of dry brown skin and exposing white flesh membrane beneath. She starts with a pearl-handled knife handed down from mother to daughter, then discards it in favour of the new one I bought last week at the Co-op, two small paring knives for the price of just one. By the fifth tiny onion her dark eyes are streaming. I stand at her left and catch tears for the stock.

Jewish partridge, we call this one, though probably the Arabs gave us the nuts, certainly the Romans brought the garum, and the clay pot belonged to my mother and her grandmother before. The meat is sweet and strong, I think perhaps you are too. They say partridges mate for life. You are a gardener and I am a cook, this should work well.

Dish follows dish, tiny bones picked and licked and sucked and cleaned. We eat small and delicate morsels across a whole day. The postman comes and goes, local bin men collect carefully piled recycling bottles and paper, black liner bags stuffed with onion skins and greasy paper napkins. I am so full. Full of her and of the day and all these months of waiting for her to come.

You do the dishes. I want to watch your Queen's Speech. My mother asked me to check it out.

Tidied house, street lights on, it's time now. We go outside. I walk barefoot on to a frosted ground, it must be truly cold for the suburb-heated grass to turn winter-crisp. I show her the shed, switch on the external lights. She is suitably impressed and turns to smile at my neighbour peering from behind tired nets. My neighbour has the gall to wave. The King of Spain's daughter pokes out her tongue. Maybe we won't be sharing next door's Boxing Day sherry after all.

Your tree is beautiful. As it should be. You are beautiful. As you should be. I am beautiful. But you knew that.

We consider dessert. A fresh golden pear, rice pudding with lightly grated nutmeg. But we are full, she and I, not greedy. Sitting in the crystal palace of my shed, me and the King of Spain's daughter at my side, we talk of her journey and the heavy water of my knowing and if she thinks she will like Brussels sprouts. I use my father's sister's recipe, cook them with chunks of salty bacon and stir in double cream at the very last minute. It's really not bad. Above us, reaching up to the glass ceiling and the pale orange sky of this old city, hang a silver nutmeg, a golden pear, and the wishbone of a partridge in a pear tree. The little tree is good to lean against, solid. You tell me your studies: Athena was worshipped as the mother of all pear trees. Perdix, one of Athena's sacred kings, became the partridge when he died – but in Badrinath, in the Himalayas, he himself was the Lord of the Pear Trees.

This tree is male-female, it carries us all.

Everyone always talks about the partridge, don't they? As if that were the point being made, the lone partridge, waiting hungrily for his life-long mate. No-one really thinks about the tree, how the precious fruit would grow, where the bird would land if the tree wasn't there. But I do, I planted it.

You planted it. It called me to you.

And now it holds us up.

INDEX OF CONTRIBUTORS

ANGELA CLERKIN

Angela Clerkin is a writer and performer. Her screenplay *Head Over Heels* is currently under option, and she has two plays in development. As an actor she has appeared in *Holby City, The Office, EastEnders, My Family, Dalziel & Pascoe* and *Sugar Rush*. Angela has just been told all the pretty girls live in south London and so is moving there.

KAREN MCLEOD

Karen McLeod is author of the award winning *In Search of the Missing Eyelash* published by Jonathan Cape. She is a recently retired Air Hostess and now works as the Writer in Resident at the Bookseller Crow Bookshop in Crystal Palace. She is a Cabaret Comic whose act has recently included performing as a six foot fish finger.

karenmcleod.info

SOPHIA BLACKWELL

Sophia Blackwell is a performance poet who has featured at Glastonbury, the Edinburgh Festival, and London venues such as the Soho Theatre and the Roundhouse. Her debut poetry collection, *Into Temptation,* is available from Tollington Press and her writing has been published in *Diva, Trespass, Pen Pusher, Fuselit* and *Rising*.

STELLA DUFFY

Stella Duffy has written twelve novels, more than forty short stories, and eight plays. Her latest novel, *Theodora,* was published by Virago in 2010. In addition to her writing work, Stella is an actor and theatre director. She lives in south London with her wife, the writer Shelley Silas.

stelladuffy.wordpress.com

VG LEE

VG Lee is currently working on her fourth novel *Always You*. Her short story collection *As You Step Outside* was published by Tollington Press in 2008. She is also a stand-up comedienne and took her one-woman show *SHUSH!* to the Edinburgh Festival.

vglee.co.uk

MEN & WOMEN

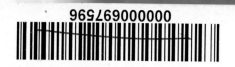

MEN & WOMEN

Edited by Paul Burston

GLASSHOUSE BOOKS

CONTENTS

ENJOY CARIOCA

ENJOY CARIOCA

PAUL BURSTON

'Take a photo of me next to that rainbow flag', Tom said. He leapt to his feet and adjusted his Speedo's.

Mark squinted behind his imitation Diesel sunglasses, quietly wondering why anyone would want to have their picture taken next to a rainbow flag. It wasn't as if they didn't have them back home in London. Rainbow flags were everywhere you went these days. You might as well have your picture taken next to a Coca Cola sign or outside a McDonald's.

'Come on!' Tom called. He was standing next to the flag now, puffing out his chest and holding in his stomach. He'd become more than a little obsessed with his body lately. He said it was because he wanted to look his best in the wedding photos, but Mark wasn't so naïve as to believe that all this effort was purely for his benefit. Tom had always enjoyed the attentions of other men. They both had. Though when it came to the wedding reception, their friends were under strict instructions not to say anything that might embarrass them in front of their families. Persuading Tom's father to attend had been hard enough, without his mother having to explain the concept of an emotionally-committed, legally-binding, non-monogamous relationship.

The rainbow flag was one of half a dozen which marked the gay section of the beach at Ipanema. Tom and Mark had been here every day for the best part of a week.

'We're here every day', Tom told the flyer boy he was chatting with yesterday. 'Every day. We went to that club last night. Maybe we'll see you in the bar? Or we'll be here tomorrow. By the flag. Yes, we're here every day'.

Mark had been busy planning this trip for months, and now they were finally here he found it a little frustrating that they hadn't ventured beyond the nearest beach. But at least they were learning to fit in. They wore Havaianas and drank caipirinhas. And after committing the ultimate faux pas of bringing towels to the beach, they were now each in possession of a kanga, which were cheap to buy, dried easily and could also be worn as a sarong. Tom's had a black and white design and the word 'Ipanema', while Mark's had a picture of Christ The Redeemer. He may not have taken the train up Corcovado and witnessed the world famous statue close up, but he had at least been sitting on its face for the past few days.

And it wasn't as if the view he was currently faced with didn't have its compensations. Around them, locals and tourists mixed together in a scene straight out of a photo shoot by Mario Testino. Men posed in tiny swimming trunks, squeezed themselves into miniature deck chairs and huddled in couples on the sand. Beyond the gay zone, people observed the usual rules of engagement and were spread out at a fair distance from one another. Inside the perimeter, there was barely room to move. As Mark reached into his beach bag, he kicked sand over a muscle guy sleeping a few inches from his feet.

'Not the phone!' Tom hissed. He waved his arms and made an exaggerated facial expression, the way English speaking people often did when surrounded by foreigners they assumed to be incapable of reading even basic body language. The expression said that taking the iPhone out on a crowded beach was a security risk. Far better to use the camera.

Mark returned the iPhone to his bag and dug around until he found the camera. It wasn't exactly cheap, but it wasn't nearly as expensive or as difficult to replace as Tom's precious iPhone. And at least if the camera was stolen, there was no chance of the thief adding insult to injury by running up a huge phone bill. He tightened the draw strings on the bag and wound them tightly around the arm of his deckchair. He removed his sunglasses and hooked them on the edge of the bag.

By now, Tom was beginning to lose patience. Mark knew this because as soon as Tom became even slightly bored, he had a habit of shifting his weight from one leg to the other. Although in the present circumstances he could just as easily have been drawing attention to his thighs. Tom had always been proud of his thighs, and justifiably so. He had the kind of thighs that were common among male sporting professionals and extremely rare among men whose only exercise revolved around the gym. Mark took a moment to admire them and felt his irritation slip away.

'Ready?' Mark called.

Tom rolled his eyes.

'Smile then.'

Tom smiled. The camera clicked.

'Take one more for luck.'

'I've taken two,' Mark lied.

'Take another one', said Tom. He smirked. 'Three's better.'

Not now, Mark thought. We're supposed to be on honeymoon.

Mark was 38 and Tom was 35. Everyone said that they were perfectly matched, though what people actually meant by that usually depended on which side of the church they sat on. At the wedding – which wasn't in a

church, and wasn't strictly a wedding but a civil partnership - their straight female friends insisted on saying how handsome they both looked, while a few of their gay male friends made subtle digs disguised as compliments. 'That suit really flatters you, Mark', or 'Have you lost weight?'

Mark hadn't lost weight. In fact, he'd gained weight. It wasn't a huge amount, but it was enough to make him feel constrained in his wedding suit and conspicuous in his swimming trunks. He envied the Brazilians with their buff bodies and narrow waists, drinking beer and snacking on bags of biscuits, making it all seem so effortless. For the past week he'd been trying to tone up a bit, jogging along the beach before breakfast and limiting himself to fruit and coffee until lunchtime. But then the afternoon would come around and his resolve would weaken and all his efforts would go to waste. For Mark, life was a constant battle between self-discipline and self-indulgence. Self-indulgence usually won. And self-flagellation usually followed.

It was okay for Tom. Not only was he the younger of the two, he was also the better looking. Mark was under no illusions about this. He had the kind of face women found handsome and gay men found interesting or attractive, depending on how much they'd had to drink, what drugs they'd taken, and how determined they were to ingratiate themselves with his boyfriend. Tom, on the other hand, had the kind of looks that demanded attention whatever the circumstances – blond hair, blue eyes, and a body that looked good in a Speedo's, even on a beach full of Brazilians who didn't know the meaning of body fat.

Mark had often heard it said that beautiful people were the most insecure. If this was true, then Tom was not one of those beautiful people. In the five years they'd been together, he had displayed very few signs of

insecurity. He certainly craved attention, and he sometimes fretted over the appearance of another fine line or another grey hair. But he wasn't prone to moments of crippling self-doubt. He wasn't conflicted the way Mark often was. He didn't punish himself. Tom lived for pleasure, pure and simple. He didn't stand by weighing up the consequences of his actions while other people had all the fun. He threw himself into things.

Yesterday, for example, he'd thrown himself into the sea – despite Mark's misgivings.

They'd been warned that the tides at Ipanema could be treacherous, that there was a powerful undertow. In fact, according to Mark's guidebook, the name Ipanema was derived from an Indian word meaning 'dangerous water'. Yesterday the sea had been particularly choppy. There were even flags - proper flags - warning people of the dangers. But that didn't stop Tom. And even when he was caught by a wave, knocked off his feet and swept half way along the beach, he laughed it off. 'This is Bruno', he said when he finally re-emerged, supported by a hunky Brazilian with a shy smile and a tattoo of some saint or other. 'Bruno is a life saver!'

Sometimes, Tom's fearlessness was endearing. And sometimes it was a little irritating.

'Look at him', Tom said. 'He's hot'.

Of course he's hot, Mark thought. It's high summer in Rio. We're on the beach. It's forty degrees. Everyone's hot.

'Is he the one from the bar?' Tom said.

Mark lifted his head from his book. 'What, the one with the plucked eyebrows?'

'No, not him. That one over there. With the beard'.

Men with beards were a particular source of fascination to Tom lately. Mark wondered if this was his way of preparing himself for middle age. He also wondered if he would suit a beard. He'd grown a goatee once, back in the days when everyone had one. But his boyfriend at the time complained that it scratched his face, and he decided to shave it off before his facial hair came between them. Too late, as it turned out. Maybe now was the time to reconsider?

'Well?' said Tom.

Mark looked, but he couldn't see a man with a beard. He could see lots of other men. There were men with shaved heads and tattoos covered in sun block. There were men sitting in their deck chairs with cans of beer and caipirinhas. There were men standing at the shoreline, facing out to sea and casting sideways glances behind their sunglasses. Then there were the men who sold the beers and the sun block, and spent their days trudging back and forth with homemade ice boxes hanging from their shoulders, display cases tucked under their arms or huge bags of cashews balanced on their heads. The beach was the main destination point for locals struggling to make a living, charging that little bit extra for a chilled can of beer or trying to persuade some big muscle queen from Miami that what he really needed was a henna tattoo and a shell necklace for his girlfriend. Most of the beach vendors were straight, though the man who sold pineapples was camper than Carmen Miranda, and the boys offering full body massages were only as straight as people wanted them to be.

'Too late,' Tom said.

Mark looked at him. 'Sorry?'

'The guy with the beard. He's gone.'

'Oh,' said Mark.

Suddenly Tom perked up. 'Oh, but look', he said. 'That other one's back again. Over there by the massage tables. Enjoy Carioca'.

Mark looked and there he was – the boy Tom had spotted on their very first day. He was a little on the short side, but what he lacked in height he made up for in other departments – broad shoulders, pert pecs, a bubble butt and biceps like coconuts. But what first caught their attention was the design of his swimming trunks. They were white, with bright red lettering across the front and back. Emblazoned across the groin was the word 'Enjoy' and across the back, 'Carioca', which Mark had discovered was the term used to denote a native of Rio. The lettering bore a striking resemblance to the Coco Cola logo, which was obviously the point, and part of Mark wanted to hate the trunks the way he hated those stupid rainbow flags. But there was no denying the fact that the boy wore them well. On lesser mortals, the trunks would have looked like false advertising. On him, the words 'Enjoy Carioca' couldn't have been more apt. He was like an exotic fruit waiting to be tasted. His trunks were a provocation. Or possibly an invitation. They might just as well have said 'Eat Me'.

'I think he's a masseur!', Tom said.

'We both know what that means', Mark replied.

'Actually, I could do with a massage', Tom said, rotating his shoulder and pulling a pained expression. 'I think I might have pulled something yesterday'.

'The only thing you pulled yesterday was that Bruno'.

'I did not!'

'Well it wasn't for lack of trying'.

'I was only flirting', Tom said. 'It was just a bit of fun, that's all.' He made a sad face. 'Did I make my baby jealous?

'Of course not', Mark lied.

'So you don't mind if I have a massage?'

'Why should I mind?', Mark said. 'It's only a massage'.

'Exactly', said Tom. He took some money from the bag and leapt to his feet. 'Right, enjoy your book'.

'Enjoy your massage', said Mark.

Tom grinned. 'Enjoy Carioca!'

According to Mark's guidebook, Rio was a city dedicated to pleasure. Yes, there was poverty. And yes, there were areas of the city that could be considered dangerous and were probably best avoided. Driving in from the airport, Mark had been struck by the favelas, which were like nothing he'd ever seen before and which seemed to stretch on for miles. And even in the wealthy tourist areas around Ipanema and Copacabana, you could turn a corner and suddenly find yourself on a side street where the buildings were boarded up and covered in graffiti and there was a possibility that you might be mugged. Desperate people did desperate things, and Rio had more than its fair share of desperate people.

But if there was one thing the author of the book really wanted to impress upon the reader, it was that the people of Rio knew how to enjoy themselves. The city had always been famous for its street parties - even before the carnival, which had its roots way back in the 1500s and was now described as 'the world's best party - period'. And despite the combination of Catholicism and machismo which ran through Brazilian culture as surely as political corruption and a passion for football, Rio was now proudly touting itself as one of the world's most popular gay destinations.

Reading this, Mark couldn't help wondering why, if Rio was so gay-friendly, so many of its gay citizens were now living in London. You couldn't walk into a gay bar in Soho without finding a beautiful Brazilian whipping up a cocktail. You couldn't go to the gay gym in Covent Garden without encountering a gaggle of Brazilians chattering away in Portugese. You couldn't venture to a gay club in Vauxhall without seeing a hunky Brazilian dancing on a podium. There was even a shop, Rio Beach, selling club wear to men whose faces and torsos were featured weekly in the gay press. Before arriving in Rio, Mark had convinced himself that all the sexually attractive gay Brazilians were now safely tucked away in London. Now he was forced to concede that there was no such thing as a sexually unattractive gay male Brazilian. And nor, apparently, was there such a thing as a sexually unavailable one.

'I'm back', Tom said.

'That was quick. How was the massage?'

Tom grinned. 'Promising'.

'What do you mean, promising? What are you grinning about?'

'You know how we said we weren't getting each other wedding presents? Well I've got you one'.

Mark looked at him. 'Please tell me you haven't'.

'I have', Tom said. 'He's going to meet us back at the hotel in an hour'.

Mark's heart sank, 'Why?'

'Why not? We're on holiday'.

'Honeymoon', Mark corrected him. 'We're on our honeymoon'.

'Oh, you know what I mean', Tom said. 'It's not like we're in London. We'll never see him again'.

Not unless he fancies a job in Soho, Mark thought.

'He's very good with his hands', Tom said. 'And he does have amazing muscles'.

Mark struggled to find a fitting description for a boy with bulging muscles that didn't make him sound so difficult to resist. 'He looks like a condom full of walnuts', he said.

Tom winked. 'Well at least we know he's safe!'

The hotel was only a ten minute walk from the beach. Mark was in no hurry to make it back, and insisted they stop for a caipirinha at the nearest kiosk.

'Are you sure that's a good idea?' Tom asked, as they sat on plastic chairs and Mark drank from a disposable cup filled with the familiar intoxicating mix of lime and cachaça. 'Remember what you were like when you had those three caipirinhas the other night. We don't want you failing to rise to the occasion'.

Great, thought Mark. Not only am I hopeless at standing up for myself. Now I'm impotent too.

In any case, erectile dysfunction was the least of his worries. One of the first things they'd discovered since arriving in Rio was that some local pharmacies were willing to sell almost anything – with or without a prescription. Tom had replenished his stock of Valium on the very first day, and on the second day they'd gone back for enough Viagra to supply a gay porn studio. Mark's guidebook was right. Cariocas took their pleasures very seriously.

'So what's the nature of our little rendezvous?', Mark asked woozily. 'Business or pleasure?'

'Pleasure, of course', Tom said. 'Like it says on his trunks. Enjoy Carioca'.

'But we are paying for the pleasure of his company?'

'I'm paying,' Tom corrected him. 'This is my present to you, remember?'

Mark forced a smile. 'I'd have settled for jewellery.'

'You have jewellery. We have our wedding rings.'

'And we're not even wearing them.'

'Not on the beach. Not with all that sun lotion. What if they fell off? They cost a fortune.'

Mark stared at him. 'You do love me, don't you?'

'What?' said Tom. 'Of course I love you. I married you, didn't I?'

'I just thought it would be different,' Mark said. 'After we were married. I didn't think we'd need anyone else.'

'Who said anything about needing?' Tom snapped. 'It's supposed to be a bit of fun, that's all. Don't be such a killjoy.'

'Sorry,' said Mark.

Silence. Then: 'Well?' said Tom.

Mark drained his cup and fixed a dim smile to his lips. 'Let's go.'

Nobody could say that the boy wasn't good with his hands, or that he didn't live up to the promise of his swimming trunks. He didn't look like a condom full of walnuts, but he did bring his own condoms and lube, which showed a certain amount of professionalism. His cock was neither too big nor too small, and he had a smooth and very accommodating ass. Mark was glad that he'd taken the precaution of necking a Viagra.

Despite this, the sex was every bit as mechanical and anxiety-inducing as he feared it would be. Not that Tom seemed to notice. Afterwards, when they'd all taken a shower together and their guest had

pocketed his money and left, Tom turned to Mark and said, 'See, that wasn't so bad, was it? You certainly seemed to enjoy yourself.'

'Of course I did,' Mark lied. 'Sorry about before. It was just . . . performance anxiety, I suppose.'

Tom grinned. 'Well you hid it well. You really gave him one.'

Mark blushed. 'I did, didn't I?'

'Hell, yeah!' Tom said in the American porn star voice he sometimes adopted during sex, and still hadn't quite mastered. 'You the man!' He gave a dirty grin. 'Maybe later, we can have a repeat performance. Y'know, just the two of us.'

Mark smiled. 'I'd like that.'

'We should go and eat first,' Tom said, pulling on his shorts. 'Keep our strength up.'

But Mark wasn't listening. 'Tom?' he said. 'Where did you put our wedding rings?'

'They're in the bathroom,' Tom replied. 'Next to my toilet bag.'

But they weren't. They weren't in the safe either. Or in the bedside drawer.

Mark felt his stomach turn. 'Fuck,' he said. 'You don't think he stole them, do you?'

'What?' said Tom. 'No, of course not.' He didn't look too sure.

'Only it said in my book that this sort of thing can happen.'

'What?'

'You know, tourists paying for men to come to their room. Sometimes . . .'

'It said that?' said Tom. 'Then why the hell didn't you say so?'

'Don't blame me,' Mark said. 'This wasn't my idea.'

Tom's eyes hardened. 'Arguing isn't going to get us anywhere,' he said. 'Let's just calm down and have a proper look.'

For the next half hour they searched everywhere – under the bed, behind the mini-bar, under the sink, in the laundry basket. But Mark knew it was useless. The rings were gone.

'We should never have taken them off,' he cried. 'I knew it was a bad omen.'

'Oh, please!' Tom said crossly, 'Stop being such a drama queen!' He paused. 'You're reading far too much into this.'

'Am I?'

'Of course you are', Tom said. 'You know you are.'

Mark stared at the floor. 'No,' he said finally. 'I don't think I am.'

LADIES

&

GENTLEMEN

LADIES & GENTLEMEN

CHRISTOPHER FOWLER

It takes a long time to truly know yourself. But knowing who you are is what the phrase 'coming out' really means. It's not just about taking a perverse delight in telling your parents that you enjoy putting an extra skip in the Hop, Skip & Jump.

One of the things writers quickly get used to doing is standing in front of a crowd of strangers and exposing themselves, metaphorically speaking. We climb onto a stage and try to explain who we are.

Every time I do it, the audience is different and the reaction is different. And one day – maybe tonight – this is what I shall get up and say.

'Ladies and gentlemen, first, let me answer the three questions I get asked most. One, yes I do write under my own name. Two, no I don't know what I've written that you've read because I'm not fucking psychic, and C, no I don't think creativity can be taught, any more than I can be taught to repair a Ford Mondeo, which apparently is a car vulgar people drive.

Also, it's insulting to be told that you thought my first novel was a career peak, and no, I never thought of myself as a gay writer, I'm just a gay man who writes.

Let me explain this last point, about the gay writing thing. By the time I started getting published, I had become embarrassed by the idea

of a gay lifestyle. As a student I attended protests and went on an awful lot of marches (why did they always have to start so early?) and eventually a reasonable amount of equality arrived – and I was there on the streets for most of it. I thought some straight kids will always hate queers, that's life, it's a balance, deal with it. Being sensitive to others is not going to compromise you. I still wouldn't go to Middlesbrough, but then I wouldn't go to Middlesbrough anyway, any more than I'd go to Afghanistan. (Actually I looked on the internet and there are a couple of gay bars there that look like nice places. They've probably been burned down by now. Middlesbrough I mean, not Afghanistan).

So it's not a perfect world, but it's better than I ever thought it would be.

But then I found an alarming correlation developing between the behaviour of gay men and teenaged girls. Both became obsessed with looks, pop, bright colours, soap operas, dancing, flouncing and pretending that nothing bad could ever, ever darken the rainbow. I thought *Boyz* and *QX* magazine were like *Bunty* and *My Guy* with cocks. I was running companies in my twenties, not spending my evenings emailing pictures of my penis to strangers.

At weekends I came out to play, but that was different. I wanted to be taken seriously at work. It seemed I hated everything gay men liked. I especially had a problem with whistles. When I went out in the evening, I did not want to look like a drum majorette on steroids.

I started my writing career as the cheesy glitter of disco ended and AIDS arrived. Bad timing, because I wanted to write fantasies, satires and mysteries, not tales about the perky upside of tragedy. Gay men were always expected to put a spin on adversity, and AIDS was a waking nightmare wherein the death of every blameless man was greeted with looks that said

'I told you so' – even within the gay community.

I didn't think sexuality surfaced in my writing. Hell, I even wrote straight sex scenes, although – a giveaway, this – I usually wrote them from the woman's perspective.

After the debris settled from the AIDS bomb we tentatively stuck our heads above the parapet – 'Oh, you're still here – Hi!' And I carried on writing through the age of the self, when everyone could finally behave like a spoiled princess. Writing about the gay life interested me even less now, because drugs had invaded more insidiously than any virus, and the pleasure of socialising with London men was destroyed by the fact that everyone was now wasted and talking rubbish.

Thanks to the internet, sex stopped defining lifestyle and we could finally be as boring as everyone else, but I still wasn't a gay writer. I didn't get an understanding of my sexuality from books, or anywhere else, although my mother did warn me I might get interfered with in Greenwich Park, which was worth making a note of. I was born in central London, so my social life was always a mix of queers and straights and everything between. Why pick just one element to write about? I read Armistead Maupin, but it was like eating beautifully sculpted icing sugar. I hoped he was predicting the future, but what once felt like an advance-party for the next century could also be seen for what it was; the liberal lifestyle of the inhabitants of a tiny, fragile bubble on the far side of the world.

As an experiment, I reluctantly wrote one gay short story. I thought it was grim and not very good, but it was accepted for a *Gay Times* anthology. There was a launch party for the book in Waterstone's Piccadilly, populated by the queeniest people I had ever seen. I stood miserably at the door watching the excitable authors scream and hug each other, and left without going in.

That's how things stayed for a long time. I wrote books and ran companies. The closest I got to writing anything gay was coming up with the poster for *Queer As Folk* – 'The Whole Love Thing. Sorted.' That was me. I didn't even watch the show.

If you're over 35 and single everyone assumes you're gay anyway. It would have been more fun to come out as straight.

When I decided to write my biographical novel, *Paperboy,* a funny thing happened as I researched it. I was shocked to realise that every single thing I had loved in my formative years was at least one thousand percent gay.

Thunderbirds.

Gay.

The Avengers.

Gay.

Jason And The Argonauts.

Gay.

Noel Coward.

Gay.

Pet Shop Boys.

Gay.

PG Wodehouse.

Gay.

Superman.

So gay.

Stephen Sondheim.

Gay.

D&G, DSquared and Agnes B.

Gay. Especially DSquared.

Federico Fellini.

Gay.

Abigail's Party.

Gay.

Norman Wisdom.

Well, that one takes some explaining.

Margaret Rutherford's interpretation of Miss Marple.

Gay.

Twiggy in *The Boyfriend*, especially when Madame Dubonnet says 'Let's face it darling, the closest you ever got to the West End was Harrow On The Hill.'

Off. The. Scale. Gay.

And my writing was gay. By now I wrote sex scenes so well from a woman's point of view that I started getting fan mail from women. I'd written over thirty books of gay. It's just that my gay was more complicated than whistles and cheery tragedy, because I was a fringe inside a fringe, not only gay but writing thrillers! Or even fringier - satirical thrillers!

Suddenly I got inexplicably angry. There's a great line in the movie *The Long Good Friday*.

BOB HOSKINS: 'You know how bitchy queers get when their looks go.'

Maybe that was what was happening to me, but I was angry because the new generation was taking it all for granted, and the price of freedom is eternal vigilance.

When the man in the barber's chair next to me started on about 'the bloody queers', I threatened to smash his face in. When a well-meaning,

decent taxi driver asked me what I thought about last night's Arsenal game, I asked him what he thought of the current production at Sadler's Wells. When Brian from *Big Brother* was quoted as saying he thought gay politics had always been boring and pointless I wanted to say don't worry, darling, we took care of all that for you, just so you can go dancing in Vauxhall without getting your fucking heads kicked in.

I went to a crime writing festival and met a coterie of blokey thriller writers who sell in supermarkets, and I saw why I annoyed them. New Men are just the old ones in better clothes, and these ones hated me for breezing in and dancing with the wives they couldn't talk to, for liking good champagne and attractive starters and Keil's moisturizer and Marc Jacobs and biceps and decent theatre seats. But most of all they hated me for stealing their language and having fun with it. I was someone to fear, the trickster, the smiley face of subversion, like the Child Catcher in *Chitty Chitty Bang Bang*. I was their worst nightmare, a faggot with money in his pocket and the confidence to fight back.

As I said, it was an anger thing. I'm over it now.

So I thought back and tried to understand the pattern of my life, because I didn't want to end up bitter and weird.

I thought back to the age of ten, and my first erotic thoughts about Superman. I thought about taking the dog for a walk in the park where young men exercised with their tops off.

I realised I was probably gay when I snubbed my school's rugby final to go to *Die Fledermaus*. Creativity is nurtured by the right time and place. I hadn't been born in either. I came from Greenwich, South London, which was the furthest our family ever managed to get from the West End. We once had an aunt who moved to Reading and we always acted as if we were going to Sweden when we visited her.

MOTHER: 'Have you got your scarf and gloves? Because it's going to be cold over there.'

Real Londoners pack food when they go to the country, just in case there's nothing to eat. My mother could rustle up a full Sunday dinner on the beach, and we were always safely back home before nightfall. Perhaps she thought we would be attacked by wolves or sold into a gypsy slave ring if we stayed on after dark.

My family fought themselves to a standstill, but I like to think I grew up pretty well-adjusted. At seventeen, during my girl-dating period, I decided I was probably gay.

ME: That's a very attractive dress.

GIRL: Really? No boy has ever said that to me before.

ME: (Thinks) Uh-Oh.

In our house sexuality wasn't really an issue because no-one ever expressed much of an interest in the subject. It was unmentionable, but so was the word 'underwear' – we always said 'nether-garments'. My mother once snogged the captain of the royal yacht Britannia by mistake (a long and somewhat unlikely story) but all forms of intimacy were taboo and anyway, nobody had the energy to think about intimacy after they'd finished a day's work. I can hardly remember a time from my childhood when my mother didn't have two jobs, so I imagine sex appeared on her agenda somewhere below rinsing the nets[1] and repairing the Ascot[2].

We had 'bachelor' family friends, and it was always assumed that if I didn't follow in their footsteps I would at least help out when they were busy. Your body was considered such a private thing that all revelations of a personal nature, from homosexuality to verrucas, were all regarded with

1. All houses in the sixties had net curtains in case anyone looked in and caught you off-guard, enjoying a relaxed moment. 2. Scary water heater whose pilot light inexplicably went out sometimes, creating panic as everyone rushed around looking for matches before it blew us all to Kingdom Come.

equal horror, thus creating a strangely level playing field of acceptability for pretty much everything so long as you kept it to yourself. Sexuality was neither very important nor interesting, because we were English and therefore above discussions about gusset-bothering. This ability and the presence of a good navy were what made our island great.

I kept my head down and worked hard at school. The twin taboos of sexuality and career occupied my waking mind. I couldn't do anything about the former, but at least I could continue reading and help advance the latter.

The sooty, partly derelict London of my early childhood was a city of ghosts. Where there are ghosts there are stories, and where there are storytellers there are actors. The London theatres kept late hours and bred their own special venues. When I was seventeen there must have been about thirty tiny theatre bars in the West End, each with its own over-dramatic personality, the Festival, the Cabal, the Rockingham. This would have been the clubland of John Gielgud and Kenneth Williams, and it was dying just as I arrived. I thought that if I frequented them, perhaps something would rub off on me, but the first Soho bar I dared to enter alone was the A&B club, and the only thing that rubbed off on me were the hairs from the monstrously fat cat that slept on the counter.

The A&B stood for Arts and Battledress. It was a schizophrenic place struggling to cope with the changing standards of the 1970s. On the one hand it wanted to be a gentleman's club which required jackets and ties, and had stained-glass crests in the windows and the evening papers neatly laid out, but it was up a disreputable red-light alley off Wardour Street and the barman had a taste for Carmen Miranda headgear.

There was something reassuring about being in a club swathed in red velvet curtains, surrounded by ladies and gentlemen who had all been in the

same production of *Aida*. Entire conversations still took place in Polari, the peculiar slang created by actors, gypsies and queens. You could be mentored by classically educated older men without worrying if they were paedophiles, and drugs had yet to rob bars of intelligent conversation. There was no binge culture. Everyone got quietly pissed and wobbled off home.

But there was a painful stiffness to the London of the seventies. Swinging London looked like your father trying to dance. I saw it in documentaries about Soho coffee bars, where a disapproving patrician would interview defensive floppy-haired chaps in roll neck sweaters and nervous girls in thick black mascara whose parents obviously didn't know they were out drinking strong coffee after nine o'clock. London might have had Chelsea and the West End, epitomized by grainy footage of a few neon signs shot at jaunty angles, but the rest of the city consisted of misty suburbs, empty roads, boarded-up lots and grimy alleys. I remember walking along the Regent's Canal and passing an upended Robin Reliant[3] sticking out of what appeared to be a rubbish-filled swamp; a far cry from the neat apartment-lined waterways that occupy the same spot today.

London existed in schizophrenic polarity. One part attended parties in the Post Office Tower's revolving restaurant while the rest watched the coverage on tiny monochrome tellies in hundred year-old slum terraces. If you want to witness the nightmare of a country trapped in two time zones, simply watch an old episode of *Steptoe & Son*, which was shot in the derelict backstreets of White City. The streets looked half-abandoned. The vestiges of wartime chaos lingered everywhere. The signs of the past, of war damage and waste ground and dingy Victorian warehouses, were not easily shaken off, and did not truly start to disappear until the early 80s.

By now Mods and rockers had been replaced by skinheads, a gormless,

3. An embarrassing three-wheeled car you could actually tip over if its driver cut you up in traffic.

bulldog-racist style born of inner-city poverty and disillusionment. One would like to think that punk evolved to oppose this movement, but the streets weren't filled with skinheads and punks attacking each other's ideologies. Punk was primarily a fashion fad centred around Chelsea, seized upon by a handful of nihilistic trustafarians who talked of revolution without ever fomenting it, and hated by everyone else except music critics who were desperate for something new to write about and art teachers who vicariously lived their rebel lives through their pupils.

English pop culture died. The sixties had bowed out on a grace note with The Beatles performing free on the roof of Apple Records, and the ensuing vacuum had been filled by tacky lounge acts from the end of the pier. As our youthful icons vanished we were left sandwiched between Morecombe and Wise[4] and the sweetly shambolic Johnny Rotten, who looked like he'd never drunk a glass of water in his life. Without role models, it's no wonder we jumped at the chance of dancing about in satin shorts to Donna Summer. The youth of the seventies had been driven into a corner, and remained trapped there by disco, which was invented solely for the purpose of allowing a DJ to put on a twenty minute track while he went out for a snout and a wee.

After my childhood officially ended at 21 (the year when you got 'the key of the door', i.e. voting rights) I hit town with the rest of the Bridge & Tunnel brigade and was photographed on the London club scene simply because I had dyed my hair Rent Boy Yellow and was wearing roller skates. When the picture appeared, I found that makeup and eye shadow had been added to the photograph by retouchers in an attempt to suffuse me with an aura of unbridled queer hedonism. It made me look like the love-child of Gary Glitter and Barbara Cartland. The picture is supremely

4. Old school comedians so innocent that they shared a bed in their sketches.

awkward. I'm spinning a girl in a silver leotard, and it doesn't look like we're having fun, it looks like I've broken her back.

London's creeping air of desperate 70s sexuality was summed up by the arrival of a gay nightspot called Adams, which hosted London's first back-room and was next door to the Odeon Leicester Square. This in itself was shocking because the Queen attended Royal Film Performances in the cinema with which it shared an adjoining wall, and her proximity to men having sex must have unwittingly duplicated life at the palace. Adams appeared at the height of the moustache-and-parachute-trousers period in male fashion history. Everyone had to act as if they were in the infantry. To prove the point, the club had a camouflaged army jeep sticking out of the wall in its lobby and phallic rockets poking up from the floor. If Donna Summer had ever appeared in an army recruitment video, she would have shot it here.

The superclubs were in their infancy and threw endless fancy dress parties, as if they couldn't believe their luck at being allowed to open, so it was still a novelty to be stuck on Tottenham Court Road at 2.00am in thick snow dressed only in Speedo's, body glitter and workboots. Wild times were nothing new in London. I have this on reliable authority from my mother, who says that if you wanted to get high in 1959, you drank three Babychams and sat through *Fantasia*.

At that time I was writing for an advertising agency, setting up a film company, trying to write my first novel, working as a freelance cartoonist for a gay magazine called *Jeremy,* and opening the catastrophic Soho nightclub Gypsy. At weekends we went on angry protest marches and rollerskated around Leicester Square with ghetto blasters, for reasons that now entirely escape me.

London was in the grip of disco. Linda Clifford, the Boystown Gang, Earth Wind and Fire, the Ritchie Family and all the stars of the Casablanca label filled the clubs with shiny happy people on qualudes. Qualudes had been invented to provide hysterical sixties housewives with a 'Quiet Interlude' – they numbed you up so completely you spent the evening stumbling into tables and woke up the next morning with leopardskin legs.

Newly invented red and green lasers shone directly into the wide, wide pupils of dancers, giving them free eye operations. Giant video screens were deployed for the first time, allowing everyone to enjoy the horror that was Tavares lock-stepping before cameras in white spangly loons. For the first time, DJs became famous for their ability to play records in sequential order. Some of them were even under thirty. Without today's draconian Health & Safety regulations, nightclub owners built raised steel platforms for dancers, who promptly fell off their stacked heels and landed on their heads twenty feet below.

As we worked late and watched the first-generation of stupefied clubbers rollerskating past our office windows, we tried to think of a way of prising their hard-earned cash away from them. I was now twenty five.

'There's a basement available in the Chinese restaurant over the road,' said Jim, my business partner in the production company I'd set up. He took a long, slow, satisfying hit on one of the super-strength Rothmans that eventually killed him. 'A nightclub. We could run it in the evenings, charge for membership, get friends to help us, easy.'

He arranged for us to view the basement. The old Chinese owner used it to store beer and beanshoots, and was happy to be rid of the smelly damp space. The walls were covered in huge paintings of Chinese warriors bending their knees and sticking their tongues out.

We called the club 'Gypsy' after our favourite film, printed membership cards and opening night invitations, paid two months' rent in advance, ordered in booze, four coloured lights on a stick, a DJ and some ancient sofas for a chillout area that looked like my nan's lounge, then carpet-bombed Soho in leaflets. Finally we hired my mate Roger to be the barman.

'There, that's done,' said Jim proudly, looking around at the transformed Frith Street basement. It looked like a Chinese takeaway full of traffic lights. I was unnerved; we were now deep in debt, and had no assurance that anyone would turn up.

Then the gangsters arrived, in the form of a weaselly little man in a raincoat, like a character actor from a bad British comedy, who pulled up a barstool, helped himself to a large whisky and insinuated that he would be happy with a few hundred quid a week, depending on how well we did. But it turned out he wasn't a gangster, he was a genuine Soho copper on the take. We agreed to pay him his money, anything to get rid of him, and prepared to open our doors.

Thanks to the 70s love of all things disco, our opening night was insanely oversubscribed. We had queues of desperate young men and women going all the way down the street. Our barman became so inebriated that when anyone asked him for a gin he handed them the bottle and said, 'Help yourself, darling,' before passing out under the counter. A flock of spectacularly attired drag queens – de rigeur to ensure any successful opening – swept about the place in feathered headdresses, with the startled attitude of flamingos that had been deposed from an African lagoon and deposited in a damp Soho basement.

The music got louder. The temperature rose. We had no air vents. I wondered how soon it would be before people started dying. I tapped my

watch and nervously looked for Jim, who was drifting about with his hands in the pockets of a double-breasted white jacket, like Rick in *Casablanca*. I indicated it was closing time and he shrugged – how could we clear out so many people when they were obviously having a great time at our expense?

For the next month we shot past our closing times and kept the party going around the clock. We raised our entry prices to try and keep people away, but nothing would stop them from forming lines outside. It was all about sex, of course. England had been slow to catch up with the US club scene. While the so-called beautiful people on Santa Monica Boulevard were shovelling coke and burning out in the end of days, English clubbers were passing around a brand of cough syrup that was supposed to be a bit speedy.

Because we had no insurance, I stayed up late night after night to make sure the place didn't get destroyed, and crept into work shattered the next morning. The ridiculous hours soon took their toll on everyone except Jim, who seemed to be thoroughly enjoying himself. We couldn't lose money even with the barman nightly giving away all the stock.

I suppose the mistake we made was staying open right through Easter, which was apparently illegal. The weaselly policeman decided that we weren't paying him enough. 'Right,' he said, wandering around on Sunday morning and waving at the flamingo-people wrapping themselves in the decorations, 'The Queen's on her way to church at Balmoral. Have some respect. Close this lot down.'

'Do you want a gin and tonic?' asked Jim.

'No I bloody don't!' shouted the weasel. 'Turn the music off, shut the bloody bar and stop those people dancing!'

'Well,' Jim said, cheerfully lighting a Rothmans as the last of the booze was confiscated, 'that was fun, wasn't it?'

The music was about to stop everywhere. Back at the office, we were working on a film called *Discoland,* but by the time it went into production, disco was suddenly as dead as Donna Summer's reputation, so the title was changed to *Discoland: Where The Music Never Stops,* and finally, with an air of desperation, *Can't Stop The Music.*

When we saw the finished cut, our jaws dropped. The film had dated badly before it had even opened. It was impossible to imagine who director Nancy Walker thought she was making her magnum opus for. Walker was an old chorus girl from films like *On The Town,* and had filled the film with gay men and old broads, which probably reflected her life.

The wrong-headedness of this film gave a clue to the kind of dead-end in which the gay 70s now found itself. Steve Guttenburg ran around shrieking in cut-off denims, and the Village People appeared with some 8 year-old boys dressed in chaps and cockrings. For the film's doomed premiere, the distributors decided that we, the marketing men, should surrender our last shreds of dignity and show up in tiny shiny shorts and roller skates. Unfortunately the cinema had a steeply raked floor, so that when the ridicule began we found ourselves unable to move without shooting down to the front of the theatre and vanishing into the organ pit. The audience laughed with the desperation of cancer-stricken children at their last panto.

Was this the last flowering of gay freedom before the grim pandemic of the 80s? I'm not so sure. For Londoners, weirdly, it was a time of naïve joy and brotherhood. You felt connected to everyone else because for better or worse, we were finally deciding our own futures. We were growing in

confidence day by day. Our choices had yet to be usurped by the corporate world. It felt as if, for the briefest of moments, we were in control.

Now it all seems very long ago. In fact, now that I live in a world where I get more emails from my moisturiser than my extended family, it seems like another planet entirely. But I like the world now. I like being inside myself and looking out at the young, and I try not to be cynical because everybody deserves a chance. Everybody.

So, here I stand as a middle-aged gay man slightly unable to believe his luck, and if you thought this was another coming out story, then perhaps I disappointed you. For me there was no sense of coming out, but a process of evolution that incorporated sexuality with a hundred other things, including:

Learning to be fair.
Learning to grow up.
Learning to be happy.
Learning to be good.
Learning to decide.
Learning to take control.
Learning to stay curious.
Learning to say yes.
Learning to love.
Learning to teach.
And learning to learn.
Ladies and gentlemen, thank you.'
That's what I would say. Maybe I'll say it tonight.

BLISTER PACK

BLISTER PACK

NICK ALEXANDER

I am standing next to Hugo when I meet David. Which is part of the reason I go home with him I guess.

Hugo has taken my heart and fed it through a document shredder this past summer by constantly flirting with me, occasionally kissing me, and then reliably and repeatedly returning to his boyfriend.

Of course I should know better than to fall for someone who is already in a relationship, but my heart – no matter how much I argue with it – will not listen to such logic. Hugo is funny, Hugo is cute, and he only ever has to shine that electric smile of his upon me for any sensible resolve to vanish.

Tonight, some part of me thinks that seeing me go home with his friend is no more than Hugo deserves, and that perhaps the seed thus planted will grow into the jealousy required if Hugo is to finally realise that he is in love with me too.

It doesn't, of course, work.

We have been drinking since five pm – this was originally supposed to be a simple aperitif, but with Hugo things invariably overstep their boundaries, so our aperitif has morphed, drink by drink, into an all night bender.

So I am drunk as hell, too, which is probably the second reason I go home with David.

Not that David is unattractive – he isn't. He is a tall, fit-looking, swimmer's build, red-headed thirty-year-old with a goatee beard and piercing blue eyes.

But going home with a guy I have just met isn't something I do anymore. Like that Fairground Attraction song, a foolish past has left me wanting the next time to be 'Perfect'.

At least, that's what I have promised myself.

It is two am by the time we leave the pub, and if the truth be told, I am having trouble standing. Hugo heads off to his boyfriend's place and when it turns out that David lives just around the corner from me we decide to drunkenly negotiate the city together.

A few bus-swaps later we stumble onto the pavement and David says, 'Can I offer you a coffee?' which makes me snigger, because 'coffee' so doesn't mean *coffee,* and yet a coffee is so what I *really* need at this point.

I follow him down some side roads and along a dark alleyway that smells of piss, and finally across a small courtyard and up three flights of stairs.

His flat would be big enough to be impressive were it not such a mess. Every surface is covered with junk: dried up dinner plates, piles of books, a cocaine sprinkled mirror, and even some random banknotes strewn across the sofa.

David makes a vague, drunken attempt to tidy some of this up, but soon gives up and simply pushes the various items occupying the sofa onto the floor. 'Sorry it's a mess,' he says, 'but this is how I live,' which at least strikes me as honest.

He vanishes to the kitchen, and returns not with coffee, but with a bottle of vodka and two glasses. I think that vodka is the *last* thing I need.

He sits down beside me, close enough that our thighs touch, and sloshes vodka into both glasses before raising his in a toast. Through politeness, I follow suit.

He downs his drink in one and then starts dabbing at the grains of cocaine on the mirror as I sit and pretend-sip at my own glass.

'Sorry,' he mutters rubbing his finger against his gums. 'I'm out of coke. I haven't even got any GHB left.'

I shrug. 'It's fine . . . ' I say. 'I don't . . . anyway . . . '

And then he grabs my hand, stands and quite literally hauls me through to the bedroom.

He pushes me sideways and my shins hit the edge of his bed causing me to fall onto the heaped duvet in the middle.

I fidget, attempting to move the mound from beneath the small of my back, but David is already on top kissing me deeply, and after a vague initial feeling of unease prompted by the fleeting realisations that a) he doesn't kiss as well as Hugo and therefore is *not* Hugo and b) I have decided not to do this anymore; I give in, melt into it all and kiss him back. It feels good, and as we rip our clothes off and I see how ripped his body is, it feels even better.

I think, 'God, why *did* I give up on this again?'

The reason of course, is that every date for years has been a disaster movie. But here is the proof that it can feel good.

David says, 'I need to piss, don't move,' and pulls himself up and stumbles out of the room.

I blink hard in an attempt at focussing more clearly on my surroundings and glance around the room.

On the wall opposite is a Communards poster I remember from my college years. I'm quite impressed that David has even heard of them.

In the corner, nestling in a pile of clothes, I spot for the first time an overweight ginger cat. He looks like Bagpuss.

I look at the bookcase and spot a couple of novels I like, and realise that I could actually have something in common with this guy.

On the bedside cabinet I notice a half-empty blister pack. I turn it towards me so that I can read the writing: *Trizivir™ GSK.*

I sigh deeply and roll back into the middle of the bed and stare at the ceiling.

If this were the first time I had ever slept with an HIV positive guy, then it might have taken some time for any emotional response to form, but the truth is that we forty-somethings have been living with this for almost as long as David has been alive.

Blister pack, 1987:

I hold Chris in my arms. He has lost so much weight that it has become almost impossible to hold him comfortably – his bones stick out so much that it feels like hugging a tool-bag.

A nurse bustles into the room and I make to move from the bed, but she blinks at me slowly, kindly. 'You're OK,' she says, then to Chris, 'Time for another pill.'

She pops the pill from the blister-pack and hands it to him with a cup of water.

'What's this one?' I ask.

'Antibiotics again,' she says. 'Hopefully to get that lung infection under control.'

Chris renders a phlegmy, heaving cough as if to demonstrate her point before tipping his head back to down the pill. His shoulder blades dig into my chest.

Once the nurse has gone he says, 'Do you think it's true about Liberace? Do you think it was Aids?'

I shrug. 'I don't know,' I reply. 'I guess. That's what everyone's saying.'

'I don't think I want Liberace for company in heaven,' he says.

'Oh, I don't know . . . a little light piano music,' I say.

Tears well up, but luckily Chris can't see them. I swallow hard but do it slowly so that he won't feel it. 'Anyway, if you don't want to spend time with Liberace, don't join him,' I add once I think that I have my voice back under control.

'I don't *want* to . . . ' Chris says. 'I want to stay here, with you. You know that, right?'

'Of course babe,' I say. 'You'll be fine, you'll see.'

But I somehow know that he won't. I can sense that this is his final lap, and this knowing is so emotionally punishing that if there were any way to *not-cope* instead of going through it all, we would both choose it. Because nothing has prepared either of us for this. No-one ever expects to have to deal with death at twenty-three. But there is no other option, so cope, we do. Go through it all, we do.

Blister pack 1990:

Steve grasps his hot-chocolate with one hand and pushes the pack of pills around the table with the other. 'I don't know what to do,' he says. 'They make me feel worse. I think they're killing me. I kind of feel like I'm better off taking my chances.'

'I really don't know,' I reply, sipping my tea.

Everyone is talking about how toxic AZT is. In fact the side effects are so bad that plenty of people are saying that it is actually a conspiracy to

wipe out gay men. But it is the only drug available, and the truth is that I don't fancy Steve's chances without AZT either. He has lost so much weight already, he is starting to look like Chris did just before the Kaposi appeared on his cheek. Which was just before the PCP took over his lungs. Which was just before he drowned in his own body-fluids as I held him, weeping.

'I might wait until I get some really serious symptoms, and *then* take it,' Steve says. 'That's what Adam has decided.' Adam is Steve's partner. They both have Aids.

'I thought Adam had symptoms already,' I say.

'No . . . no, we think it was just the flu actually. He's fine now.'

I shrug and nod. 'Well that's good news at least.'

'But then Adam's blood counts are better than mine. Maybe I *should* take it. The doctor says I should, but I kind of feel like a guinea pig. I kind of feel like he doesn't really know any more than I do.'

'I'm sorry babe,' I tell him. 'I really can't . . . you know . . . have an opinion. Only you can make that call.'

'I know,' Steve says, then, 'Oh, what the fuck. It's die if you do, or die if you don't.'

He pops a pill from the pack and takes a swig of hot-chocolate.

Blister pack 1997:

Adam pulls them from his blazer pocket, pops out a pill and washes it down with beer.

'Are those the new ones you were on about on the phone?' I ask.

'Yeah, Combivir,' he says.

'Well it looks like it's working for you,' I reply. And it *does*. We all

thought that Adam was going to die a year ago – he even planned his own funeral – and then the drugs suddenly took a leap forwards, and here he is having a pint in Comptons.

'The side effects are bad,' he says. 'I don't like to be too far from a toilet if you know what I mean. But that's the price you pay I guess.'

'You're putting on weight though, despite it all,' I comment.

'Yeah. I feel pretty good,' he says. 'I started working out again too.'

'It shows.'

'The miracle of science,' Adam says.

A silence falls between us and I realise that we're probably both thinking the same thing: that if these drugs had arrived just a few years sooner, Steve – his partner, my friend – and Chris – *his* friend, the love of my life – might both be standing here now.

'So are you still off to Lanzarote?' I ask to squeeze that thought from the air between us. Because the weight of history that it creates is always just too much for any of us to bear.

I sigh and glance back at blister pack, 2011.

Because I have held a lover as he died of Aids, and because I have had friends declare that they were newly infected with the virus and because I have dated and slept and lived with guys who were HIV positive and because I have gone for countless tests myself and nearly fainted with relief each and every time that they confirmed that wearing a condom and being careful around bodily excretions really *is enough to keep the virus at bay,* my emotional responses are all ready and waiting. And despite my drunken state, they fire off immediately: I feel sorry for David for having to live with

a life threatening illness. I wonder how a thirty-year-old could be stupid enough to *catch* the disease. I wonder if his treatment is working for him. I wonder why he hasn't told me and wonder if he *should* have told me. I wonder if the pills on the side are, in fact, his *way* of telling me.

But most of all, I feel suddenly exhausted. Because Aids is ultimately just so fucking boring. It's like a miserable TV drama that just goes on and on and on, day in, day out, for your entire life – only the TV set has no *off* switch. And whether you have the disease or you don't, you still have to worry about it constantly.

And it would just be so nice if, just for once, I could have a kiss and a cuddle without that particular cloud of impending doom hanging over my head – hanging over the bed.

This sudden feeling of emotional exhaustion isn't particularly conducive to sex, it has to be said. Motivated by a desire not to offend poor David who clearly has enough on his plate, I instantly decide to stay and go through with this. I always have safe sex anyway, I figure, so what difference does it make?

But despite that decision, the simple reminder of that great ogre Aids – an ogre that has been wrecking my and my friends' lives for the last thirty years – is not something that makes me feel particularly rampant.

David returns and throws himself back onto the bed and starts kissing me again, and I let him do this and try really hard not to wonder what might come next, and what his viral load is and whether I have any ulcers in my mouth at the moment, and . . . and . . .

And I notice a strange chemical taste in his mouth now, a previously undetected bitterness in his body odour. Is it just the remains of the cocaine, or can I actually taste the Trizivir in his body?

He pulls my jeans off and glances at my limp dick and then stands and hops out of his own jeans. His dick stands tall and proud. 'Mine's ready even if yours isn't,' he says with a cute laugh, and then he jumps back onto the bed, kneels before me and pushes my head down.

I take his dick in my mouth and perform some mental gymnastics and somehow manage to remove the theoretical-but-generally-agreed-to-be-infinitesimal risk that oral sex carries from my thought processes.

'Ah yeah, that's good,' David says, sounding suddenly like a low-budget porn star. 'Yeah, take it down boy.'

As he says this he starts ramming his dick down my throat which makes me gag and actually hurts a fair bit, and the thought comes back: 'is this safe?'

And then my mouth fills with the taste of his pre-cum, and suddenly I am *unable* to forget.

I pull away from him and fight the desire to run and rinse my mouth out, forcing instead a smile. I start to kiss him, but he keeps trying to force my head back down again. After a third attempt, he freezes, frowns at me, and asks, 'What's wrong?'

'Nothing,' I reply, smiling.

He shrugs and grasps my head trying to push it down again.

'Nah,' I say, resisting. 'Kiss me.'

But David pulls away. He looks annoyed. 'I thought you were enjoying it,' he says.

'I was, you have a lovely dick. But now I want to kiss.'

David crosses his arms defensively. 'Something's up. Tell me.'

'No, nothing's up.'

'I don't believe you.'

'Ok . . . It's just . . . look. I can taste pre-cum,' I tell him, attempting to combine the declaration with my cutest shrug.

'And?'

'And . . . I don't like tasting pre-cum.'

'Right. Because?'

'Look. I know that you're positive, and I'm not convinced that it's safe. But it's fine, we can do other . . . '

'Who the fuck told you that I'm positive?' he asks, turning red now.

'No one told me. Your meds are on the table,' I say, reaching out in an attempt at stroking his arm – an attempt that fails because he flinches away from me. 'And that's fine, but I'm not comforta—'

'Fuck you!' David mutters. 'How fucking *dare* you try and make me feel bad!'

'Look, it's fine David. Calm down and we can just . . . I just don't want to suck you off, that's all.'

'And I don't want to do *anything* with you. Jesus. In 2011.'

'In 2011 what?'

'I can't believe that people still behave like *you*. In 2011.'

Feeling suddenly vulnerable I reach for my jeans and start to wriggle into them.

'So what, you're going to fuck off now as well?' David spits.

'No!' I reply. 'I just . . . want . . . my jeans. Just fucking calm *down* will you?'

'You can't even catch it like that.'

'It's very low risk. Sure. But it's not a risk that I'm prepared . . . '

'In fact you can't catch *anything* from me, because as you so rightly spotted, I take my fucking meds.'

'That's good David. That's great. But I don't know you that well, and I can't leave my health in your hands. I have to look after *myself*. You get that, surely?'

'So you don't even *trust* me now? It gets better and better,' he says, snidely.

'For fuck's sake David, will you just ... ?' But my voice peters out. Because David has left the bedroom.

I cover my mouth with my hands and sit silently for a moment before standing and – realising that I am suddenly sober – pulling on the rest of my clothes.

In the lounge David has returned to the sofa and is sitting beneath a blanket caressing his cat. He looks very small as if he has somehow folded his athletic body away.

'Look, I'm sorry if I hurt your feelings,' I tell him. 'I really didn't mean . . .'

'Hurt my feelings?! Fuck you!'

I shrug. 'Maybe I should just . . .' I nod at the door.

'Nice,' David says. 'Classy. Come here. Insult me. Then fuck off.'

'Look,' I say. 'I can't seem to make this better. So maybe that is the best thing.'

'No you look. I mean, what do *you* know about HIV?'

'I'm sorry? What do *I* know?'

'*I* have to live with the virus,' he says. 'I have to live with the guilt. I have to remember every day to take my meds. I'm the one that has to go to the hospital to check my viral load. And if on top of that I have to put up with cunts like you who think you can catch HIV from a fucking blow job, well . . .'

'But you *can*,' I say. 'There is a small but real risk. And I often take that risk. But not when someone who I know to be positive is ramming his

cock down my throat, and not when I can taste cum. Those three together aren't a very sexy combination for me. I'm sorry, but they aren't.'

'You're so fucking ignorant. That's what gets me. The Swiss Study showed that . . . '

'Don't even go there,' I reply, starting finally to feel quite angry myself. 'I'm a fucking journalist. I write for fucking *Health Now*. So I know all about the Swiss study, so don't even try . . . '

'Which *showed*,' David continues pedantically, 'that you can't even catch HIV from someone who is taking his meds.'

'No! Which *showed*,' I say, now raising my own voice, 'that in a *heterosexual monogamous couple* with *no* secondary infections, having *only* vaginal sex, where one partner is successfully taking combination therapy *and* has had an undetectable viral load for over a year, that the risk of transmission appears to be unmeasurably small. So unless you have a vagina and want to marry me it doesn't actually say that much about what's happening here today.'

'So, suddenly you know more about HIV than I do. That must feel great,' David says.

'No David. Not *suddenly*,' I say, struggling to sound reasonable. My anger at this arrogant thirty-year old who apparently thinks that he is the world's expert on HIV, simply because he *has it*, is rising, and if I don't get away soon I may lose control here.

'I have known a lot about HIV for far longer than anyone should ever have to,' I tell him, my voice quivering, 'and that knowledge has kept me *safe*. And I'm really sorry you have it, but it isn't actually my fault.'

'Fault? Well it isn't my *fault* either. Yeah. before you ask, he told me he was negative. So it wasn't my fucking *fault* either.'

'He told me he was negative,' I think. *'He told me it was safe.' 'He told me he was taking his meds.'* When were these ever reliable enough to stake your life on them?

'And I don't need your fucking sympathy either,' David says. 'So don't be sorry.'

'I'm mainly sorry you were so determined to ram your cummy cock down my throat despite having HIV . . .' I think, but thankfully restrain myself from saying.

'I think you should leave,' he says.

'Finally. We agree on something.'

I grab my coat and wrench open the door, but I suddenly feel terrible. I suddenly feel like I have become the aggressor here. I remember Chris, and Adam, and Steve, and see David as a simple historical extension of our long-suffering past.

I glance back at him. He is staring at me, tears streaming down his cheeks.

'I'm sorry David,' I say. 'I'm *really* sorry.'

'Fuck you!' he spits back, weeping now. 'And *Fuck off!*'

And with the thought that nothing I can say or do will, tonight, fix this for any of us, I shake my head, and step out into the stairwell and start to descend the stairs.

Outside, it has started to rain, the courtyard is cold and shiny.

I cross it and head back along the alleyway and out onto the street, and wonder what exactly has gone wrong here tonight, and indeed what exactly has gone wrong since nineteen-eighty-three that this should *still* be going on, that we should *still* be having to deal with this shit almost thirty years on.

Aware of the taste of cum in my mouth and with an almost hysterical desire to get rid of that taste, I walk briskly homewards.

As I round the end of my street my phone beeps with an SMS.

It is from Hugo. 'What the fuck have you done to David?' it says. 'He's a wreck. I'm going to have to go round there. I can't believe you sometimes.'

I pause for a moment, the rain trickling down my back as I try to think of a reply. And then I slip the phone back into my pocket and carry on towards home.

Because the truth is that I don't know what I have done to David.

I really don't have the faintest idea.

THE ANNIVERSARY

THE ANNIVERSARY

ALEX HOPKINS

Frank was fuming. Ben was late.

Sipping his second large glass of Pinot Grigio, he surveyed the scene around him like a jaded Bette Davis.

It was a hot summer evening and all of Soho was out. The air was brimming with lust and Frank had had to fight his way through the crowd to find a seat. No sooner had he done so than yet more people arrived, milling around in their Abercrombie & Fitch, flexing their muscles and demanding to be admired.

Frank's diminutive figure was totally obscured by the heaving mass of bodies. It was a scenario guaranteed to bring out the worst in him; he quickly isolated a focus for his distaste: a bulking Muscle Mary in an improbably tight red vest. The crisp wine burnt Frank's forty-Rothmans-a-day throat as his eyes narrowed and bore into his prey.

Ben eased his way through the crowd with a confident swagger as Frank stood and bellowed through the nameless faces in his finest Norma Desmond intonation, 'You there! Why are you so late?'

As Ben approached Frank looked him up and down scathingly, registering his red eyes and sickly pallor. 'Hello Velma,' Ben said shyly, using the nickname he had affectionately given Frank years before.

'I have been waiting here, amongst this rancidity, for almost half an hour, dear,' Frank spat. 'Clearly you were out on the shame last night – *again*.'

'Well . . . ' Ben began, taking a seat at the table.

'Don't tell me,' Frank interjected. 'A night of unspeakable carnage at the sauna! I can smell it. But surely today of all days you could've been on time. You know how I fucking hate this place. And sitting here on my own like some aged hooker really is quite lamentable.' Frank rasped deeply on his cigarette.

'Sorry, Velma.'

It was the anniversary of Frank's late partner's death. It had been a year since Frank had returned from his job at the hair salon to find Blake lying on the bed in a pool of blood. His alcoholism had finally taken its toll and Blake's small, pale body had been stuck to the red sheets like a slaughtered animal.

Ben had been the first person Frank had contacted the next morning, and, in an act of kindness that Frank would never forget, the 28 year old had phoned all of Blake's friends to break the news.

Ben had first met Blake years before, when Blake had chased him around a pub in Romford asking him if he fancied being photographed.

Tonight they had met to remember.

Frank refilled his glass and turned to glare at the crowd. 'Look at this lot, strutting around like rancid peacocks,' he said. 'It makes me sick! Look at that one there,' he continued, prodding Ben's hand and gesturing towards a man in a red vest leaning languidly against the huge glass window. 'She's been there an age, dear, propped there, waiting to be picked 'n' poked.'

'Oh leave her . . . I mean *him* alone,' Ben said. 'He's not hurting anyone. Anyway, he's quite hot.'

Frank slammed his glass down on the table. 'Hot? Hot!' he exclaimed. 'That's all any of you queens ever think about. Never mind what's inside.

Oh yes, I've seen it all on that Gaydar dear. N.S.A., hung only, straight acting. *Please!*'

Ben shrugged.

'The problem, dear,' said Frank, grasping Ben's hand, 'is that people don't talk to each other anymore. They'd sooner send some wink on a computer screen while they flick their bean.'

'I know,' sighed Ben, 'but it is as it is.'

'Well it wasn't like that in my day,' Frank muttered. 'Mind you, Blake would have loved it. A quick way to get cock.'

'Oh Blake always knew where to find the boys and the booze,' Ben recalled fondly. He scrunched out his cigarette in the ashtray, rubbing the stub around thoughtfully. 'When did he actually *start* drinking?'

'Oh, he always drank, dear,' Frank replied. 'It started when his mother disowned him for being gay, I think. Rich coming from her, a former chorus girl. Her legs went up with a fluency of their own.'

'My parents were fine when I came out,' Ben said.

'It was different back then,' Frank said solemnly. 'Drinking kept Blake's demons at bay.'

'I can understand that,' Ben said.

'Of course you can, dear,' Frank squawked.

'What do you mean?' Ben said defensively, avoiding Frank's glare and looking towards the guy in the red vest.

'Oh for fuck's sake do you really think someone like that can bring you happiness?' Frank barked.

'I wasn't thinking anything at all.'

'You were thinking about cock. Just like Blake always did. Jesus, gays are their own worst enemies.'

*

The street was now seething with people and a doorman repeatedly had to pull them back from the road to allow cars to pass. No sooner had he done so than the bodies spilled forward again, carefree and oblivious to danger.

Frank twisted the top off another bottle of wine as his eyes darted back towards the guy in the red vest who had just been approached by his mirror image: another Muscle Mary in his mid thirties. Rage swept across Frank's face as he noted that they had their hands on each other's arses.

'Well that didn't take long did it? Like attracts like!' he exclaimed.

Ben looked puzzled.

'Have you left your contacts in the sauna as well as your dignity, dear?' Frank asked.

Ben frowned.

'Two minutes into meeting and they're practically licking each other out,' Frank raged. 'Disgusting!'

'What's wrong with it?' Ben said.

Frank puffed extravagantly on his cigarette and blew the smoke into Ben's face. 'Won't last though, dear. Never does.'

'Well, maybe they know each other. I think you're being unnecessarily harsh, Velma.'

'And I think you're being naïve, dear,' Frank retorted, taking a huge gulp from his glass. 'In my day people exercised a bit of caution when they met. We had romance.'

Frank began to laugh to himself. 'Oh when I think back to how Blake and I met,' he said, breaking into a tender smile. 'There I was, walking down the promenade minding my own business. A beautiful young thing – just 18. Oh, and I *was* beautiful: slender, toned, what you might call a natural beauty. Not one of these steroid queens you get today.'

'Anyway,' he continued, 'there I was, gazing out to sea, when I sensed a car slowing down beside me. Curb crawling.'

'Oh I say,' Ben said, urging Frank on. 'What did you do?'

'I carried on walking of course, but I stole a glance and noted that my pursuer was in a spanking new Rover. Very glamorous to a lad from Boscombe Bay I can tell you.'

'Oh I bet,' Ben said, smiling.

'So I slow down slightly, as does the Rover, and turn to the left to grab a gander at the driver . . . '

'And?'

'Well, obviously, I'm hoping to see some gorgeous Latin type, but instead I'm greeted by a prematurely balding, gruff looking creature with the most pronounced jowls I have ever seen on a man under eighty.'

'Blake!' Ben laughed.

'Indeed, dear,' Frank drawled. 'Well, obviously I looked away at once. Let's just say the old minge did not twinge. So I carried on walking. A lot faster I may add.'

'And what did *he* do?'

'What the fuck do you think he did? He continued to chase me of course.'

Ben let out a guffaw of laughter and then conscious that he sounded like a latter day Kenneth Williams, quickly checked himself.

'But then,' Frank went on, 'I hear the voice! It's like they had on the BBC back in those days, rich and authoritative. Oh, Blake had such a fabulous voice.'

Frank sat upright in his chair and pushed out his chest. 'Do you want

a ride in my car, young man?' he booms. 'No I do not', I reply, marching onwards. 'Are you sure?' comes the voice again. Well, at this point I stop dead in my tracks and turn to face those legendary jowls. 'Will you please stop pestering me you lecherous man,' I cry. You have to remember I was most respectable back then, dear.'

'Of course you were,' Ben winked.

'But then something rather unexpected occurs,' Frank added. 'My eyes move down from that less than appealing face towards the arm resting so manfully on the side of the open window.'

'And?'

'Well then I noticed . . . '

'Noticed what?'

'The hair, dear! The hair! Oh, his forearms were so magnificently hairy. I am afraid I was done for. The voice, the hair and the brand new Rover shattered my decorum and in I jumped.'

'And that's how it all began,' Ben concluded.

Frank shrugged. 'Yes, dear. That's how we all met back then. That is called playing hard to get.' He smiled. 'Not the sort of thing that happens in your saunas I should imagine.'

'No,' replied Ben.

'It was exciting back then. The risk made us feel strong. Brave pioneers,' Frank said shooting another glance over towards the two Muscle Marys who were now kissing.

'Disgraceful,' he said. 'Not like in my day, not with my Blake. Well at least not at the beginning,' he murmured ruefully.

*

Inside the bar, huge TV screens flashed with images of intimidatingly perfect underwear models as the Brazilian bar staff continued, with customary nonchalance, to serve the five deep queue. The incessant thud of the music spilled out onto the street adding to the aggressive undercurrent of desire that punctuated every conversation.

A morose silence had temporarily fallen between the pair as they stared at the empty bottles of wine and the overflowing ashtray.

Another muscle clone fell into their table and Frank was once again stirred into action. 'For fuck's sake,' he snapped. 'Have these people no shame?'

'It is as it is,' said Ben.

'Will you fucking stop saying that?' Frank squealed. 'It's an outrage!'

Frank's voice rang around the street and Ben shuddered with a mixture of mirth and embarrassment. He looked on with horror as a vile expression crept across Frank's brow.

'Well, well, well,' said Frank in his finest Crawford twang. 'Look what we have here.'

'What?' Ben asked.

Frank pointed a witch-like finger towards the two Muscle Marys. 'Over there.'

Looking, Ben saw that they had been joined by another guy, sporting a faux-hawk. He was about Ben's age and although he had clearly been going to the gym, was not yet the size of the other two.

'Well, that says it all, dear,' Frank exclaimed, sounding pleased with himself.

'How do you mean?' replied Ben.

'Oh get with the program you silly queen. It won't be long before

they're in a push-me-pull me – probably on that traffic island over there.'

Ben looked more closely at the threesome. 'Actually, she . . . I mean *he* looks rather familiar.'

Frank raised his eyebrows scornfully. 'You know your taste never ceases to amaze me. Another spa conquest I take it?'

Ben looked again at the faux-hawk and nodded, 'Yes, definitely him.'

'Dimensions?' Frank persisted.

'I don't recall,' Ben said. 'It was dark. And I was on plant food.'

'Yes, and I bet her soggy bed needed some feeding,' Frank muttered. 'Does she have a name?'

'No one really exchanges names there, Velma.'

'No, I don't suppose they do,' Frank snorted, waving his glass in the direction of the younger guy, now standing between the two hulks.

'And her only souvenir from *that* coupling will be a drip tray the next morning,' he seethed.

Ben looked at Frank with disgust. 'Must you be so coarse, Velma? He seems sweet to me.'

'Coarse? Coarse, dear? Coarse suits this lot like a feather boa suits Burley Shassey.'

'Well it is as it is,' Ben said for the third time.

'Stop saying that,' Frank hollered, 'It *is* what you fucking well *make it*.'

Ben looked Frank squarely in the face. 'Oh come on, Velma, you and Blake were hardly faithful to one another.'

'She was the one who couldn't keep her python in her trousers. What did you expect me to do?'

'Two wrongs don't make a right,' said Ben quietly.

'How dare you judge me!' Frank snarled. 'Were you there? Did you see what I was put through? Did you see what he brought into my home?' Frank twisted his head towards the window. 'All *I* ever wanted was . . . '

'What?' Ben asked.

Frank shook his head. 'Nothing . . . Another drink, dear.'

He sipped his wine and then continued, 'The reason I have such contempt for compulsive shaggers like this lot, is because of what it did to me and Blake. Oh God, I was innocent back then. She whisked me off that fateful day and I thought I was walking into some romantic idyll.'

Frank tapped the rim of his wine glass 'This got in the way from the start,' he said. 'We quickly became the Taylor and Burton of Harrow, but it was at a party about six months into the relationship that I knew for certain what I had got myself into.'

'Picture the scene – a divine sunken living room in Chelsea. Now, I had been keeping a close eye on Blake all night – last seen propping up the bar with some scantily clad Swedish floozy I recognised from a party at the Royal Opera House. A shameful gathering *that* was too.'

'Oh God,' Ben interjected.

'Anyway, I'm ensconced in a scintillating conversation with the legendary Bette Bourne and a particularly loathsome Quentin Crisp clone who keeps trying to steal my thunder, when I see that Blake has vanished, complete with Miss Sweden.' Frank puffed on his cigarette as Ben waited for him to continue.

'Slithering up the stairs like the canny Margo Channing I am, I go off in hot pursuit. *Fuming* I may add! Reaching the top of the marble staircase, I note something of a commotion coming from the silken boudoir opposite. Flustered queens everywhere dear! And what can only be described as a queue.'

'A queue?' Ben asked.

'A queue! Well, of course I go in, dear. Oh, you wouldn't *believe* this room. Palatial would be an understatement. Anyway, as I stand under these unfeasibly luscious chandeliers I spot the bed – a great gilded row-boat of a thing, floating about four feet off the lush shag-pile carpet. Well, the next thing I see . . . '

'Oh no,' groaned Ben with a look of horror.

'Let me finish, dear,' snapped Frank. 'The next thing is see is a mass of moaning, contorted bodies all over the bed. Utter carnage. And then right in the middle of it all, dominating the scene like some withered harlot at one of Emperor Nero's orgies, is Blake.'

'Anyway, on top of Blake, riding him with the ferocity of Lester Piggot in the final stretch of the grand national is the Swedish tart.'

'Jesus what did you do?' Ben said.

'I waited,' Frank said, smiling in a malicious way.

'So . . . I wait until Miss Sweden has screamed and jolted her way to the most frenzied climax I have ever seen and then I *attack!*'

Frank put down his glass abruptly and stared into Ben's eyes. 'I grab the rancid knob jockey by her filthy blonde locks and slap her hard across the face. She squeals and scrambles off the soiled sheets before falling into some stranger's groin – mouth open, naturally.'

'And Blake?' said Ben.

'He looks at me and says, 'Oh don't be such a silly queen, come and join us.'

Frank placed both hands on the table in front of him. He looked like a gazelle about to spring into action. 'The next sound was a resounding punch followed by a piercing scream as I thrust my fist into Blake's gob.'

'I can't imagine how much that hurt you,' Ben said quietly.

'You have feelings, Ben. You can,' Frank whispered.

*

It was now ten pm and one of the Brazilian bar boys had began to fold the tables outside the bar. As he approached, Ben saw Frank's face redden.

'Oh why don't they just sweep me up and dump me over there with the rest of the trash?' Frank said.

Taking Frank's arm, Ben led him to one of the remaining vacant spots. Frank tottered precariously and had to lean against the window. Ben had rarely seen him look so vulnerable.

'How did you move on from there?' Ben asked.

'We didn't,' Frank said, his voice hollow. 'We just existed in a sort of limbo. Comfortable despair. The drinking became worse, and one tart after another . . .'

Frank stared into the distance taking in the surrounding anonymous bodies that would either go home alone or find some brief solace in the arms of a stranger. He looked blankly over this alien world where he knew he did not belong. A siren screeched over the noise of the crowd.

'It was after the arrival of that vile junkie, Diego that I knew it was the end. Blake had seen that Brazilian bitch lurking around the cat food in Morrison's, you may recall, and had engaged him in a titillating conversation about pussies.'

'I remember the day it all fell apart with him: I had moved to Sonya's across the road so I watched the shenanigans from her window. Blake was parading up and down the street in her dressing gown as Diego smashed

car window after car window. The police arrived and carted her off. She was screaming and banging the inside of the van. And then Blake fell to the pavement managing somewhat miraculously to keep his glass upright.'

'Oh Velma,' Ben said, gently placing a hand on Frank's shoulder.

'Of course Sonya told me to stay inside,' Frank continued, 'But I ran across the road to him. He was lying on the steps, a leaf clinging on to the deep gash on his forehead. I cradled him as he looked up at me and softly cried, 'Come back to me baby. I'm sorry.''

'And you went back,' said Ben flatly.

'You know I did. He knew I would.'

*

Ben reached out to the window to steady himself. He sank to the tiny plinth between the window and the street and stared at his feet.

'Are you ok dear?' asked Frank.

'Yes, yes.'

'What is it?'

Ben continued to look at the floor. He felt Frank's hand on his head. 'Nothing. It's just, well, if that's what love is like, I don't want any part of it.'

Frank's hand began to softly ruffle Ben's hair. 'That was what *our* love was like,' he said. 'Yours doesn't have to be that way.'

*

Flier boys were moving through the dispersing crowd; lonely figures were drifting off with these advertising cards in their hands.

Frank took a final gulp of his drink and placed his glass on the ground. It was promptly knocked by a stray foot and smashed into pieces. Under his breath, he began to sing *Strangers in the Night*. A young boy of barely sixteen, his shoulders hunched, walked down the street accepting every flyer offered to him. At the end of the road, he froze. Frank watched on impassively as the boy solemnly opened his hands and let the brash leaflets fall into the gutter like confetti.

'So you off to the spa again, dear?' Frank asked.

'Probably. And you Velma?'

'Oh I shall wander home and jump on the Gaydar, dear.'

'Well you never know, you may find the man of your dreams.'

'No. I've had my time. I'll just have a gander at the pictures, dear. Easier that way.'

'Easier?'

'No talking. No risk. But don't learn from *me*,' Frank warned.

It was then that Ben became aware of three voices, the only conversation he could make out above the cacophony.

'Great to catch up with you tonight mate. It's been too long.'

'Yes, you're not wrong there! And I'm so glad it's worked out for you two. Who'd have thought it, eh?'

'Where you heading now?'

'The sauna I reckon.'

'We're so glad that's behind us, hey Dan?'

Cautiously, Ben raised his eyes from the pavement, aiming them at the three pairs of feet that stood before him. Tracing the strong legs, he lifted his gaze until it met the three men they had been watching all evening. The two older Muscle Marys clung to each other fiercely.

The faux-hawk was staring at them in awe. 'I hope to see you both again,' he said.

'Defo. Come over next week.'

'Next week?'

'Yeah. We're having a party to celebrate our first anniversary.'

'It's your wedding anniversary?'

'Yeah. Well . . . our civil partnership anniversary. We'd love you to be there.'

'I'd love to guys. Thanks.' He then hugged them both and began to walk off.

'And be safe at that sauna!' one of them bellowed as he began to weave his way down the street.

Ben looked at Frank and saw that he was crying silently. Tears were streaming down his face.

'That was all I ever wanted,' Frank said, his voice breaking. He reached out a shaking hand towards Ben. 'You queens today don't know how lucky you are.'

'You really think so?' Ben said. 'Has anything really changed?'

'Yes,' Frank replied, blinking the tears from his eyes, 'Yes it has.'

He stared into Ben's face. 'You have a choice now. That's what's changed.'

*

As Ben left the bar, he turned once more to look behind him. Most of the people had now left and were wending their way to a late night bar, a club, or a sauna – the choices were endless.

Ben saw Frank walk slowly into the distance and descend the steps of the same tube station he had used for the last thirty years. Just ten yards behind Frank were the Muscle Mary couple walking hand in hand, a picture of fearless solace.

Ben moved on down the street, his head swamped with images: he saw Blake and Frank together the day they had met; he saw Frank throwing his head back in joy as he strode down Bournemouth promenade with Blake in happier times; he saw the unconditional love on Frank's face as he gathered Blake up from the ground. And then he saw himself in his immediate future: a dark cubicle, another nameless partner.

Ahead of him, Ben saw the faux-hawk from earlier walking hesitantly down the street as people spilled from the bars. Ben sped up and began to follow him, keeping a watchful distance. He saw the boy turning towards the sauna. He saw him pause outside the entrance to the place where Ben had spent so many lost nights.

Ben held back and waited. The young guy stood still for a few moments before evidently reaching a decision. Looking at the entrance to the sauna one last time, he instead crossed the road and kept on walking.

Moments later Ben reached the same spot. He stopped. He looked up towards the sauna's door. He raised his head high and smiled to himself. The young guy was still in sight ahead of him.

Frank's words echoed in his head. 'You have a choice now.'

Ben crossed the road too and walked briskly on.

FERN COTTAGE

FERN COTTAGE

WILLIAM PARKER

Good God – What a ridiculous carry-on! Anyone would think I'd taken a knife to the bloody boy. That damned woman who calls herself 'Senior Warden', Mrs. Calverley, has just barged in and interrupted my breakfast to announce to me that the whole business is to be discussed at the weekly meeting of the Governing Council. Bloody interfering old busy body. I'm not having it – I'm just about at the end of my tether. It's too ridiculous, it really is – one may as well be back at school in Winchester in the bloody thirties, the way they're going on. 'Governing Council'! Damned charity do-gooders with nothing better to do than terrorize defenseless old men and women, that's what they are. What the hell do they think they're going to do about it anyway? Expel me? Pack my bags, dump them at the front door and order me a taxi? Jesus Christ.

This is a goddamned awful place, it really is. Three months of hell, it's been. It's a wonder I'm still alive. I'm not a particularly demanding person, but I can't tell you how many times I've asked them to bring me quite ordinary blankets and sheets for this bed. Blankets and sheets. Is that really asking too much? The bed in itself is not that uncomfortable, but they've given me something called a 'duvet' – apparently all the rage everywhere for the last three decades. It very well might be, but it's bloody well passed me by. A duvet's a sort of great bulky continental quilt of a thing that they

spread across the bed, but that's not anchored in any way whatsoever to the mattress. This means that the infernal thing moves around all night long of its own accord like a demented badger, leaving me, at least two or three times a night, completely uncovered and forced to embark on a hunting expedition in the pitch black to try to ascertain its whereabouts. Damn bloody thing.

I'll tell you something quite honestly – they can bloody-well send me packing if they want. I'd be glad to get out, I truly would. It's difficult to begin to describe the full horror of the goings-on in this bin – the duvet is one thing, the atrocious food, another. Yesterday at lunch we were presented with jelly and cream for dessert – the jelly with not so much as the slightest passing reference to any type of a flavour whatsoever. It might pass muster with the old crocks with no teeth, but really! After the insult of the jelly and before I had time to leave my seat, we found ourselves being regaled by someone suffering from the delusion that he was some sort of 'entertainer' – a dreadful magician type person flicking playing cards through his fingers and pulling yards of red handkerchief from his pockets for bloody hours on end. I managed to escape halfway through, but unfortunately not without a bit of a scene taking place. My usual seat at the table by the window is some way away from the door, and on my journey across the room, I somehow got my bloody zimmer frame caught up in Lady Chisholme's dressing gown. Hell of a fuss about that, with a great wail going up from the old trout because her bad foot somehow became involved, but they managed to get me out of the damned room as quickly as possible to avoid a real ruckus. Luckily, Jamsheed – my only ally in this godforsaken place now that Ahmed's abandoned me – was on lunch duty, but took time off to guide me along the corridor back to my

room as quickly as he could. He's a very patient young man, a damn good sort. 'First the zimmer in front, then Mr Lord Toby following, first the zimmer in front, then Mr Lord Toby following, first the zimmer in front, then Mr Lord Toby following ...' Just can't get used to the damn thing, and why should I try when I'll be dispensing with it in the next week or two? Bloody nuisance, that's all it is. It'll be thrown out into the corridor as soon as this hip stops behaving badly. But thank God for Jamsheed. Patience of a saint – or a fakir or gin or whatever passes for a holy man in Bangladesh. He must know about the Ahmed business of last night now, though. I suppose it's all round the place. Just hope he doesn't listen to what they're saying and take against me. Brought me a cup of coffee earlier and didn't seem off key with me, so that's quite a good sign.

Anyway, got back to the room after the Lady Chisholme incident, and slammed the door shut. Didn't mean to, actually – just a momentary loss of control on account of an altercation with the zimmer. Jamsheed giggled and pushed his fingers into his ears and whispered 'Matron comes to tell you bad boy!' Before he left, he patted a few cushions and propped me up into my armchair and then helped me put on a CD of *La Stupenda* – may she rest in peace – at full volume on the earphones for half an hour. Last act of *La Traviata*. Sublime noise. Blessed escape from this wretched place for a while. And then, just as I was trying to get a bit of a nap, the old bugger from across the corridor started up. Same thing every damn afternoon I've been here. Top of his voice. 'I want to go home. Tell my mother to send her car round for me! I must have my mother's car! Let her know I'm here ...' Two hours of it with his door wide open until I'd really had enough.

'Excuse me,' I shouted, 'Could I ask you how old you are?'

Exasperated reply after a pause. 'I'm ninety two! Ninety two!'

'In that case, might I be permitted to ask how old you think your bloody mother might be now?' That shut him up for a bit.

But all that was before the misunderstanding with Ahmed last night. Oh Christ.

I should never have left the house in Smith Street. Never. The whole thing's been an absolute disaster. Barbara's doing. She was so bloody persuasive, always going on about 'you know I'm talking sense, Toby…' Barbara's our family solicitor. I inherited her from my brother Dickie, and he inherited her from Father, and it's possible the link goes even further back than that. Goodrich and Eastley. Founded in the 1830s, I think – at least, the Eastley part was, so they've been around for generations. Not Barbara herself, of course – the girl's only in her early fifties and is the newly appointed senior partner.

Warden's just been in. Conciliatory tone's been adopted. She's not so terribly rotten, actually. Put her hand on top of mine and I let it stay there for a bit. I suppose I rather overreacted myself this morning, what with the unjust accusation and the general tone of being told off. She's now saying this will all be settled between herself and the staff and therefore there really is no need to take it any further. So no Governing Body nonsense at the end of the week. But she did say there were to be changes in my care that we'll have to talk about later today. Bloody embarrassing and unjust, of course, but better than what was being threatened before. I thought I'd better tell her I'd spoken to Jamsheed this morning after breakfast and had arranged for him to help me pack after lunch, but she seemed surprised by that, since he's just finished his shift and isn't due back until the day after tomorrow. Anyway, I'll get her to tell him not

to bother now that the issue's on the point of being resolved. Little bit relieved, actually.

There's nowhere for me to go, anyway, so less than no point in my storming out. Barbara has sold the house, so returning to Chelsea's not an option. Oh, she's not told me that, of course, about the house. We've never had an honest conversation about it. But I'm not yet so senile that I haven't worked it out, and I've signed so many bits and pieces of paper recently that one of them was bound to be a sale agreement. Remember the story of Queen Elizabeth signing Mary Queen of Scots' death warrant, pretending she didn't know what she was doing and then accusing her advisors of making decisions behind her back? Same sorry tale here. I've signed the house away, quite obviously, and all my bits and pieces are in storage. It had to be, of course. This place costs an unbelievable fortune, so Barbara's had to raise the money somehow. Eight hundred pounds a week. Yes – truly. Absolute daylight robbery. But somewhere along the line I seem to vaguely remember seeing the figure of over a million connected to Smith Street, so I suppose this bin's affordable as a result. But can you imagine – over a million for a two up, two down workman's cottage in Chelsea! The place cost me £5,000 in 1947, borrowed from dear Mother. Well, that seemed an absolute fortune at the time, but the cost of things now! Oh, I suppose my addled brain's not keeping up. I can't get used to anything new. I'm being left behind – the world's changing so fast. These days I find the best way through is to pretend that one's above it all, that one really can't be bothered to take it all on board – the spiraling cost of living and emails and laptops and mobile phones and cheques going out of fashion and a million channels more than you could ever need on the TV. Basically, I'm

such an old luddite that I'm only just about up to speed with the idea that steam can be made to push things along, but I'm a bit lost with everything that comes after that, and frankly I'm sure it would be just the same if I were forty years younger. But there are extraordinary things going on now, changes that make one feel as though one's living in a science fiction novel. My brother Dickie has only been dead fifteen years, but he'd call me a fantasist if I was to try and explain to him that it's possible now to have a machine in your car – a tiny screen – with an officious sounding woman telling you to 'turn left and turn right in a hundred yards and then full speed ahead but mind the speed camera' and on and on, all the way until you reach your destination! 'Sat-nav', I think they call it. The whole thing done from satellites in space. Quite incredible.

But let's be brutally honest now that things seem to be calming down here after the business of last night. Even if the house was still there, I wouldn't be able to manage the stairs. Bloody hip and the trouble it's caused me. I actually heard it go when I was walking out of the marquee at my great-niece Charlotte's wedding. 'Plink, crack' it went, and then terrible pain and all the rest of it. That was eighteen months ago. I've had a new joint put in – it's a year now – but I'm still unsteady on my pins, and no one is quite sure why. Should have bounced back by now, but haven't. Just got to be patient with it, that's all. Hip operation, followed by some fiery bug picked up at the hospital which apparently went on a sort of munching rampage round my body, and then a urinary infection and catheters and pneumonia and months of being nursed back from death's door before coming here.

I never did go back to the house. Would have had a better look at it and said goodbye if I'd known it when I was locking the front door for what

turned out to be the last time. The whole hospital thing's affected my mind, too. Forgetful now, sometimes dreadfully so. Doctor came in here a week or two back and wanted to do what he called 'an assessment'. Asked me who the Prime Minister was! Bloody cheek, but could I come up with the bugger's name at that precise moment? Not a chance. Could see his face, though. Young chap, sort of goody-two-shoes type, not sexy.

But you know, if I'm being honest, the thing I miss most of all now that I'm an old codger, is the cottage down at Lessington – even after all this time. Nearly thirty years now. I miss it more than Smith Street really. I do actually think Giles would have let me keep it if I'd struggled a bit harder – he knew how much I loved it, and the memory of his parent's links to me would have made it difficult for him to ask me to give it up. But after he succeeded his father, I knew he'd be wanting it back – his sister Nancy has it now – and besides, there was no John anymore and dear old Vere went into such an immediate, steep decline as soon as he died there was absolutely no point in going up to the dower house to see her. Perhaps Giles felt I should be making more of an effort with his mama, but I really did find the whole thing frightfully difficult. Then that journey through south London became a frantic bore once everyone decided it was their God given right to own a car. Mitcham High Street and its damn sari emporiums for hours on end – unbearable. It all became rather depressing – being in the cottage and knowing I ought to pop up to see Vere who no longer knew who the hell I was. And no Carlo of course, by that time.

Anyone who knows me must be aware that I'm the most unsentimental of people, but Carlo had become such a presence down

there that without him it just wasn't the same. No John, no Vere and no Carlo. I started missing weekends and one day suddenly realized that I'd not been for two or three months and that the garden would need a real seeing-to – then it occurred to me that the tiny rent I was paying was money down the drain, which was rather stupid thinking really. So I allowed it to slip away. Now it's like the memory of some precious family heirloom that it seemed a good idea to sell, only to find out too late that you ache for it. Oh dear, the regret around it all. But regret or not, it would be quite impossible now – the stairs were even narrower and steeper than they were in Smith Street, it's far out in the depths of the countryside and quite impractical for an elderly gent.

Yes, I'm overly sentimental about Lessington and dear old Fern Cottage. In fact, I think it's true to say I'm more sentimental about things and places than I have ever been about any person, living or dead. It seems my heart's quite capable of pining for the memory of frost on a topiary box hedge in an English garden in winter or a view of some sun drenched Italian piazza, the memory of a beautifully sung lieder recital or a Poussin masterpiece – but when it comes to people, I miss no one. Really. It's the most extraordinary thing, but I've always seemed unable to shed a tear over those who have gone ahead of me. Just as well, too, since nearly everyone I know is dead now. I don't have the facility in me to mourn; no death has ever torn my guts out. I don't really know why that is, but it's the plain truth.

I'm exaggerating a little. I remember receiving the news that Carlo had been killed. I have an image of myself pressing the receiver to the side of my face, staring, as though hypnotised, at the rug in front of the fire in the cottage whilst absentmindedly and rather bizarrely wondering about the

people who'd made it, their lives spent spinning and knotting the wool into shape in some distant mountain village in Turkey. I remember the dash to London to comfort his distraught sister, driving through country lanes, for some reason singing at the top of my voice. I remember organizing a funeral with great efficiency and steeling myself for an invasion of hysterically unhappy Sardinians, and I remember being all things to all men for those wretched few days, never too busy not to be able to offer a shoulder to cry on, always around with a hanky to dab away at a shower of tears. As though I was a hired mourner, touched by nothing more than a professional concern. It was the only way it could be, though. Yes, now and again, there was a squeeze to my arm, a slightly embarrassed hand applying an uncertain rub to my back – a tacit acknowledgement of something. 'This is Toby – great friend of dear Carlo's. He's been an absolute stalwart …' was the way Susanna chose to introduce me to the English cousins. But I didn't encourage anything else. And I survived, of course. Carlo's a distant memory, his grave destined to go unvisited now that my hip so troubles me. Incredible that he's been dead for nearly thirty five years now.

Perhaps it was the war that turned off something in me. I don't know. Others have fared just as badly, with just as much tragedy. All those boys in the trenches in the Great War – youngsters from the classes just a year or two above my brother Dickie at Winchester, with their CCF games suddenly turned real. Swathe after swathe of young men reaped for nothing and now forgotten. And then, just a few short years ago, no war, but that vicious disease for which there was never any hope of a reprieve until recently – no walking wounded, even, just the absolute certainty of death. 'I'm sick of fucking funerals – I'm never going to another one. I'm going to party, party party!' That was what the young waiter with the ring

through his nose who used to work in the Chelsea Kitchen said to me in the middle of it all. He'd had enough of crying, and he was frightened, too. Who the bloody hell could blame him? A version of those hellish trenches for modern times.

My war was fought from the airfields of Kent. That's how I came across my little refuge.

'Why don't you take Fern Cottage, Toby? It will save you motoring back up to London when you don't feel like it.' Old Lord Horsham, John's father, offered it to me, and I jumped at the chance once we'd walked over and he'd shown me around. 'All frightfully basic, I'm afraid – no mod cons, but you could make it quite comfortable without much effort, I expect …' It was good of him too, since John was a new friend from Oxford and I was on my very first visit to Lessington. The place was quite unfurnished, and Mother obliged by sending down a van full of stuff taken from the attic of the London house – everything used, everything useful and everything fitting in as though made for the place. Never had to buy a thing for the pantry, because the housekeeper up at the big house would always make sure there were essentials in the ice-box, even when they weren't certain I was going to be there – a kindly contribution to the war effort, with not much regard to ration quotas, either – always a few rashers of bacon and a sausage or two wrapped in greaseproof paper on a white plate. It wasn't only me they kept an eye out for – part of the big house was given over for the duration to servicemen who were recuperating before going back to the front.

In the early days, all through the war, I'd spend as much time there as I could – I preferred it to ever being in London. In the winter months,

I'd light the fire and stare into it for hours on end with Ptolemy, my daft poodle, curled up on my lap, clicking his mouth and licking his lips with blissful satisfaction. On summer days, as soon as I'd arrived, before even unlocking the front door, I'd be stripping off my shirt, spilling out of the car and throwing myself down into the long grass in front of the cottage. I'd fall asleep, allowing myself to believe there was nothing else in the world but the cottage, the sun in a blue sky warming my skin, birdsong, the smell of the grass beneath me taking my weight, my much loved MG, with its door still open after my hasty exit, engine clicking as it cooled down after my race through the countryside, and Ptolemy. No war, no death.

It was hellish. Of course it was. A lot of us were on automatic after a few months. No better than robots, doing what was required of us. I suspect it was the only way of getting through the muddle. But even the worst memories have softened now. When you're an old man, everything from the past, however traumatic, begins to bask in a golden glow, slowly turning into fond recollections. I find myself almost smiling when I recall those dusty old images, now robbed of their horror – the guttural roar of the twin engines of the Mosquito, the last hint of a sunset behind us as we cross the Dutch Coast, the crack of flak bursting all around as we near our target, Ptolemy's worried but trusting face looking up from his position at my feet in the cockpit and then the black canvas of Hamburg and Leipzig and Berlin far below us, painted red as we drop our 1,000 lb TIs to light up the ground for the Lancasters behind. Beautiful Dresden, burning bright in the far distance after we'd banked to return home, the bitterly cold thin air eating through layers of clothing as the reflection of the monstrous luminous flames searing human flesh thousands of feet below danced around the cockpit. Towards the end of the nightmare there's the

memories of the clear June, Luftwaffe-free skies above Normandy, the adrenaline rush as we dive, guns blazing, towards tank-laden steam trains and the fast moving convoys of retreating Wehrmacht Generals. And always the exhilaration of finding ourselves to be still alive, returning in our frayed, wooden framed Mossies, skimming the trees on the borders of the airfields. Then the back-slapping congratulations on surviving another mission, the debriefings in a cloud of tobacco smoke and the putting off for an hour or two the mental count of missing heads. But every morning would see empty chairs tight up against the table at breakfast, untouched knives and forks on either side of a mat, an unclaimed scarf on a peg, a motor bike outside the mess, the handlebars at an angle like the pricked ears of a dog who's waiting, listening in vain for the footsteps of his master who'll never return.

It passed me by, the sight of those empty chairs. I made sure it did. There was no other way.

Just once I let my guard down. The war was nearly over when one evening after an aborted mission I brought Charlie Byrne back from the airfield to the cottage. The only one to visit – Charlie Byrne with his dimpled cheeks, curly black hair and blue eyes. Charlie and his Jimmy Stewart impression and his non-stop flow of conversation late into the night, putting a broken world to rights. I made a bed up for him on the too small sofa and put another log on the fire to keep him warm before I climbed the stairs. 'It's cold down there, Toby…' he said to me in the early hours of a Siberian morning as he slipped into my bed and put his arms around me. He so very nearly made it to the end, but he never came back from the skies over the Ardennes just a few days later. January, 1945.

I'm to have blankets and sheets, Maria from Romania's to be my new care assistant and Jamsheed will deputise for her on her days off. It's settled. All more than amicable. Mrs. Calverley and I have just thrashed it out and I'm quite happy about it now, though it will take a few days before things are running smoothly. She's promised to make sure that Maria understands that my morning coffee must be piping hot, I like it brought to me before the eight o'clock Radio 4 news and I don't want any conversation interrupting *The Today* programme. I'm not worried if bumptious Melvyn Bragg is talked over after nine o'clock when she comes back in, but not before. Those are my only rules; otherwise I regard myself as an extremely easy going sort of chap.

Ahmed had it down to a fine art. But he's decided he doesn't want to be my care assistant any longer, so that's that.

I never meant to upset the boy. I'd grown so fond of him and our talks about the changes going on in Tunis and all that might mean for the future. So much so that two weeks ago I offered him a little money to help him go home for a week or two to join in the protests and be part of the whole thing – to share in the sense of history so that in the future he could tell his children that he'd been there, at least for a part of it. But, of course, he's far too honourable a sort to have even begun to entertain the idea of a gift of money – he held my hand so firmly after I'd offered, so pathetically grateful that there's someone within these blighted walls who understands and delights in his excitement.

But it's all gone now. So stupid. In just a moment's ridiculous silliness, I've spoilt a friendship. I know he's leaving soon anyway, to go to medical school, but we got on so well that there was every chance that he'd have

become one of my regular, small band of visitors. He'd have been the youngest one, apart from great-niece Charlotte who really comes under sufferance, bless her.

After the bloody thing happened, when I saw the hurt and embarrassment in his eyes, I thought he might be persuaded to pass it off as nothing more than an idiotic senile fumbling, a momentary lapse, but I quickly saw that wasn't going to be the case and I then decided to come clean, strip away my quite misplaced pride and offer an abject apology. But still no go. Just an awful silence with him staring at the floor. When he left the room – with me still dripping wet from the shower, a towel clinging to my waist and the damn zimmer quite out of reach – I could feel myself taking refuge in a not very heroic self-justification – defensive rubbish about it being common knowledge that a young chap from North Africa could usually be persuaded to do just about anything for not much more than the odd packet of cigarettes – and how the hell was I to know that things had apparently moved on? But it won't wash. It really won't wash. It put me in mind of Dickie years ago, and his failure to see that an overture to his very pretty young physiotherapist was such an insult. 'She's an Alexander technique teacher, Dickie, not bloody Christine Keeler,' I'd said to him. 'Oh, yes, well, I know that, but everybody likes a little bit of extra cash … ' If Ahmed had been some other young chap, he may very well have had a giggle in the staff room with his workmates about an old man's unexpected peccadilloes, but that, quite obviously, isn't his way.

It was only a hand making a bit free while he was helping me in the shower. That's all. Nothing that a little slap to the wrist wouldn't have stopped immediately. But it was taking advantage. Me at my careless worst. Silly bugger.

It's been a very long time since I touched anyone, you know. And a long time since anyone touched me – apart from the times it's been necessary to tap my old bones, listen to my heart, help dress me or rub a few muscles when the hip's been misbehaving. It's been a long time since anyone put their arms around me, actually. A long time now. A long, long time.

INDEX OF CONTRIBUTORS

ALEX HOPKINS

Alex Hopkins is a freelance writer and journalist. He is Associate Editor of *Out There* magazine and has written for *Time Out, Open Magazine* and the arts website Culture24. Alex has a column in *Q:ID* magazine and regularly shares his thoughts on his blog Dissident Musings.

alexhopkins.wordpress.com

CHRISTOPHER FOWLER

Christopher Fowler is the award-winning author of thirty novels and twelve short story collections, and creator of the popular Bryant & May mysteries. He currently has a column in the *Independent on Sunday*, is the Crime Reviewer for the *FT* and writes for many other publications. After living in France and the USA he now lives in King's Cross, London with husband Peter.

christopherfowler.co.uk

NICK ALEXANDER

Born in Margate, Nick has lived and worked both in the UK, the USA and France and is best known for his self published 50 Reasons series of gay novels. His latest work, *The Missing Boyfriend* reached number one and spent more than six weeks in the top ten of Amazon's Kindle chart. Nick's entire backlist has now been acquired by Corvus and will be progressively republished from August 2011 onwards.

nick-alexander.com

PAUL BURSTON

Paul Burston is a best-selling author and award-winning journalist whose novels include *Shameless* (shortlisted for the State of Britain Award 2001), *Star People, Lovers & Losers* (shortlisted for the Stonewall Award 2007) and *The Gay Divorcee* (voted Book of the Year by SoSoGay 2010). His short stories have appeared in *Bloody Vampires* and *Boys & Girls,* which he also edited.

Paul is also the host of 'London's peerless gay literary salon', Polari and a curator at the London Literature Festival.

paulburston.com

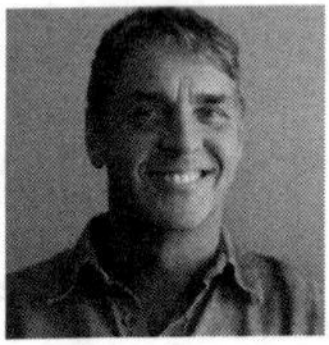

WILLIAM PARKER

William Parker was born in Newport, Gwent and spent his early childhood in the Middle East. He later trained as an actor and spent over twenty years in the profession before deciding that treading the boards was far too frightening a way of earning a living. His first novel, *The House Martin* was published in America in June 2010.

william-parker.com

MEN & WOMEN

A GLASSHOUSE BOOKS COLLABORATION

Design by Eren Butler
Edited by Paul Burston
Managed by Bobby Nayyar
Typeset in Arno Pro and Champagne & Limousines
First published 14. 07. 2011
'A Partridge in a Pear Tree' by Stella Duffy was first published in *12 Days*, Virago, 2004

ISBN 978-1-907536-11-3

Glasshouse Books
58 Glasshouse Fields
Flat 30, London
E1W 3AB

glasshousebooks.co.uk – facebook.com/GlasshouseBooks – @GlasshouseBooks
Printed and bound in Great Britain by T.J. International, Cornwall

GLASSHOUSE BOOKS TITLES 2011

WEST OF NO EAST

MEN & WOMEN

EXIT THROUGH THE WOUND

FREELANCER'S DIARY APP